THE DOG ON THE ROOF

THE DOG ON THE ROOF

A CASA COLONIAL MYSTERY

MARY MADSEN HALLOCK

CREATIVE ARTS BOOK COMPANY
Berkeley • California

The Dog on the Roof is published by Donald S. Ellis
and distributed by Creative Arts Book Company

For information contact:
Creative Arts Book Company
833 Bancroft Way
Berkeley, California 94710

ISBN 0-88739-422-1
Library of Congress Catalog Number 2002102143
Printed in the United States of America

ACKNOWLEDGEMENTS

My very special thanks to Inocencio Velasco of Oaxaca, without whom this book could not have been written, to Jake Fuchs, without whom it might never have been published, and to my brother Harry Madsen whose imagination is without bounds.

Sarah Andrews, Ken Dalton, Jon Howe and Thea Howe, the critique group extrordinaire, have bestowed unbelievably patient and kindly support.

My gratitude also to Patricia Wilson, Peggy Malliet, Lenore Mulryan, Leslie Sanders, Margaret and Cory Sonnen, Paulette Sonnen, Douglas Symes, Lene Symes, Mary Smith and Peter Kirkwood for their encouragement.

Igualmente, muchas gracias a Tomás Martínez, Candido Morales, y Jo and Gilbert Doarme.

THE DOG ON THE ROOF

CHAPTER 1

Doña Milly awoke with a start. Somewhere across the patio of her little hotel, a door had slammed like a shot. And now she heard stealthy footsteps shuffling past the lime tree just outside her cottage. She sat up in bed, heart pounding, eyes wide in the darkness.

Without thought in that panicky moment, she made an involuntary gesture toward the other twin bed. Instantly, she recalled that it was empty, that Herbert had died six long years ago and that she was on her own. Totally. She ran her fingers through her short, white curls as if pushing the memory aside to better concentrate on the furtive movements outside her door. She held her breath and turned her head slightly, her senses strained in fear.

The whispery footsteps hesitated, then veered off and moved down the path toward the veranda, gradually fading away. Milly let her breath out in a tremulous sigh.

The garden now seemed unnaturally quiet. A bird fluttered uneasily in the branches of the big jacaranda tree that overhung her cottage roof. A muted "thunk" told her that ripe fruit had fallen from the lime tree onto the path.

A tree frog gave a sudden shrill whistle, making her jump.

"Jesus!" she muttered.

At once, the impetuous frog launched into a rollicking concert, loud and reckless, as if to inform the entire city of Oaxaca that he had driven the unwelcome presence out of Doña Milly's garden and the danger was past.

"If *you're* no longer frightened," Milly told the frog in a quivering whisper, "then neither am I."

She punched her pillow and lay down again, still trembling, but confident that her household was now back to normal. She did have to wonder, though, why one of her hotel guests had been slamming doors and sneaking around the garden in the dark.

She reached out to her talking clock and pressed it gently. "It-is-two-fifty-seven-ayem," reported the familiar electronic voice.

Gradually, Milly's heartbeat slowed and once again the warm darkness became a comforting friend. After all, she was perfectly safe here inside the walls of her own Casa Colonial. With a contented smile she rolled onto her side, delighted at the prospect of three more hours of delicious sleep before the City of Oaxaca's demanding church bells summoned the faithful to early mass. When that time came, as always Milly would shower, dress, and resume her duties as Doña Milly, the *dueña* of Casa Colonial. Until then, she'd snuggle and drowse among her soft pillows and blankets.

As she hovered on the edge of sleep, a watchdog barked from his post on the flat roof of the house next door, his deep voice fierce and heavy with authority, alerting his human family and defending their territory against danger. Had he, too, heard the door slam? Milly frowned, but after a minute or two, the dog subsided.

❧ ❧ ❧

Some twenty miles to the south, when Paco Soriano López heard the rooster crow just before dawn ·it didn't occur to him that the day ahead might be different from any other. No one, he said later, not even God, could have imagined what was to come.

El gallo negro, the black rooster, announced the day to the whole village just as he always did. And Paco Soriano López, as always, rolled over, blinked, and stared out the open door into the thin light of morning. Careful not to disturb his three children or their grandfather, he arose from his straw sleeping mat and slipped into his shirt and trousers. He rolled his sarape inside the mat and stood it against the wall. Then, as a proper Zapotec should, he moved to the family altar to give thanks for the new day.

Just as he did every morning, Paco stepped outside and looked toward the eastern hills. Today the indigo pre-dawn sky was pierced with shafts of violent pink where the sun would soon appear. High overhead, creamy, rose-tinted clouds hung motionless in the sky. By mid-afternoon they would drift together, form a solid grey overcast and rain tenderly on the corn.

Paco glanced down at Amelia, his wife, as she knelt beside the charcoal fire, fanning it into life. She smiled up at him. The morning would not be complete, reflected Paco, without Amelia's gentle smile, the sound of her hands patting and shaping the *masa harina,* and the delicious odor of corn *tortillas* toasting on the *comal.* By and large, life was good and he was content.

If he had one overriding worry, it was his father. Lately, the old man's joints had been so swollen with arthritis that some days he was unable to rise from his sleeping mat on the dirt floor of their one-room adobe house. Paco wished that he could afford a bed to ease his father's pain, or at least a soft mattress to put on the floor for him.

Amelia handed Paco his breakfast tortillas and a small packet containing his lunch.

"I'll be working in the corn again today," he told her. He filled a plastic bottle with water from the well, slung his wooden hoe across his shoulders and set out along the path winding between the three dozen houses that made up his small village. Past the church, into the countryside he went, munching his tortilla.

The sun had risen now and the shadows cast by the copal trees were long and scraggly. Doves cooed in the branches, and far off across the Valley of Oaxaca a burro brayed its morning song. Paco Soriano López plodded along, enjoying the feel of the cool dust as it sifted between his bare toes.

At the edge of the cornfield Paco set his lunch and water bottle in the shade of a cork oak tree. He leaned on his hoe and surveyed his few hectares of land with a practical farmer's eye. The few spiked *maguey* plants he had put in last year were still pindling, but at least they had acquired a toe-hold in the rocky soil. The small patch of castor beans, this year's cash crop, loomed tall. The rangy plants were loaded with clusters of prickly pods, each concealing a single large bean streaked with gray and rosy red like the dawn sky. The man from Oaxaca who'd bought last year's crop had told Paco that the castor oil squeezed from those beans would probably go to the United States where it would lubricate fine machinery. It was a true mystery, thought Paco, that a bean so beautiful and so useful could also be so poisonous.

And the corn. Never had he seen such corn in this part of the valley where the soil was poor and rocky. Paco looked heavenward and thanked God humbly for what promised to be a bountiful crop.

He began his work on the row where he'd left off yesterday, removing weeds with his hoe and loosening the soil around the roots of each plant. This was his first crop of corn for the year. For once, the rains had been so generous that the tops of the plants waved higher than he could reach. He'd already pulled every third row, selling the *elotes*, the tender, milky ears, at the big Friday market in Ocotlán.

Now the final harvest was near, and in a few days he'd

4

clear the field. After that, he'd plow and put in a second planting. "Gracias a Dios," he murmured quickly, lest God send a sudden hailstorm or a high wind to punish him for his pride.

By the time Paco had worked his way only a dozen steps down the row, he could see nothing but the corn around him. He felt as if he were moving inside a pocket of warm, still air, heavily humid and buzzing with insects. He stopped frequently to crook a forefinger and scrape the sweat from his brow.

Halfway along the first row, he came across three broken cornstalks lying in the dirt. What? Had his neighbor's goat gotten loose again? Disgusted, Paco lifted the first stalk, examined the roots and wondered if he could replant it. And then, where the cornstalk had been, he saw a shiny black shoe, a trim, sock-clad ankle, and a trousered leg. Was some well-dressed man from the city sleeping off a drunk here in the cornfield?

Angrily, Paco took hold of the foot and tried to shake its owner awake. To his horror, the entire limb was as stiff as a log of firewood. It had the unmistakable feel of death about it. Ay-yi!

Paco pushed aside the other two cornstalks to reveal the body of a man dressed in expensive black trousers and a heavily embroidered *guayavera*. Paco was stunned by the richness of the clothing. The shoes alone must have cost a fortune! What was this wealthy man doing here in the corn patch, dead as a foundered donkey?

Paco forced himself to look at the man's face. Between the staring eyes was a neat, round hole and a tiny trickle of dried blood. Paco shivered and crossed himself, knowing that since the man had died by violence, his ghost would be hovering near.

A sudden puff of wind shook the cornstalks like a spectral *maraca*. Terrified, Paco threw down his hoe and ran.

As he approached the village, he slowed to a walk, panting, trying his best not to attract attention. He slipped between the adobe houses without seeing anyone and turned in at his own gate. Inside the patio, the grandfather sat on his chair, shucking corn. Amelia knelt at her loom, working on the placemats ordered a few weeks ago by Doña Milly. The two of them looked up at Paco, startled. He marched past them, staring straight ahead, and spoke out of the corner of his mouth.

"Come into the house," he said without moving his lips. "We need to talk." He strode through the door, not stopping until he was on the far side of the small room.

Amelia followed close on his heels. "What's wrong, my husband?" she asked anxiously.

"See a ghost?" asked his father with a chuckle.

Paco glared at him. "No, Father," he said, "I did not see a ghost, but it's a wonder. There's a dead man—a rich dead man—in the middle of our corn field. He's been shot." Paco plunked the end of a forefinger between his own eyes to demonstrate.

Amelia gasped and clapped both hands over her mouth.

"The policía are sure to think I killed him," groaned Paco. "What shall we do?"

"Who is he?" asked Paco's father.

"I don't know."

"Then how do you know he's rich?"

"You should see his clothes, Father! He's rich, all right." Paco felt numb. He stared at his sleeping mat, wishing he could unroll it, go back to bed and start the day over again.

With an irrepressible grin his father said, "After dark tonight, let's carry our dead visitor down to the bus stop on the highway and prop him up on the bench. He'll be sitting there waiting for the bus to Oaxaca when it comes early tomorrow morning."

Paco shook his head. This was no time to be making jokes. The older his father got, reflected Paco, the more he seemed to enjoy laughing at death.

Amelia said in her practical way, "That would bring the

federales to Santo Tomás Jalieza, Grandfather. We don't want soldiers here with their crude questions and sticky fingers. Let's ask a *brujo*, a witch doctor, what to do."

"*Muy bien*, you do that!" was the quick reply. "Paco and I will wait here so we won't attract attention by all going at once. Listen carefully, Amelia, so you can come back and tell us every word the brujo says."

Amelia rolled her eyes. "All right. Which one should I go to?" she asked in a resigned voice.

"Don Porfirio," said Paco's father without hesitation. "He's the bravest and his spells work without fail."

Amelia crossed herself three times and kissed the knuckle of her thumb reverently for luck. Then she marched out of the house and down the dusty street. Paco, watching from the outside gate, saw her smile and wave at her friend Teresa, as if nothing were wrong at all. When she knocked on the brujo's door it creaked open, Paco could hear it, and he saw her go inside.

When she emerged a few minutes later, Paco tried to read her expression as she walked toward him along the street. Amelia was brave, he thought in wonder. She was terrified of the brujo's supernatural powers; they all were! And that, thought Paco, with belated insight, was why Grandfather had sent Amelia to the brujo instead of going himself.

Amelia walked into the house.

"Well?" demanded Grandfather. "What did he say?"

"Don Porfirio's eyes grew bright when I told him about the body. I could tell that he was amazed. He said, 'Tell Paco to return to the field and hoe his corn. He should start at the far end and work back toward the body. He won't be able to finish the hoeing today, so he won't get back to the dead man before the day is over. At the end of the day, he's to go home for supper, just as he always does.'" Amelia paused and took a deep breath.

"Is that all?" asked Paco, not sure whether he felt relieved or disappointed.

Amelia held up a warning finger. "'But'," she continued, "'at midnight, when the village is sleeping, Paco must return to the cornfield and bury the body.'"

Bury it? In the dark? At midnight? Poor Paco trembled at the very thought.

"Don Porfirio says you must bury it deep! You are to use his magic shovel with the metal blade. He'll leave it by the gate for you. When you return the shovel to him, he'll erase the entire experience from your memory. The body will be gone and you'll remember nothing. This will be much better than calling the police."

"That is true," agreed Paco.

"Aha!" said Grandfather, "That brujo is a smart fellow. We'll do exactly as he says."

Paco returned to his cornfield with the greatest reluctance. First he covered the body again with the three uprooted cornstalks to protect it from the eyes of humans and vultures. Then, following orders, he took his hoe to the far end of the field and set to work. He waved to his neighbor, Enrique, who was heading toward his own plot of corn on the other side of the hill. After that, Paco tried to keep his mind on what he was doing, but all day long he was acutely aware of the richly dressed corpse lying in the middle of his precious cornfield. He was terrified of coming face to face with the *pena*, the ghost. Several times he looked up in terror, expecting to see it wavering toward him through the cornstalks. By late afternoon, when clouds covered the sun and it began to rain, he was more than ready to quit and hurry home.

Amelia had prepared black beans for supper, building her charcoal fire under the shed roof attached to the patio wall, where she'd be out of the rain. Paco spied a bit of meat in the pot. Instead of dividing it equally, as the proper head of a Zapotec household should, he kept it all for himself. If he were to be up digging half the night, he reasoned, he'd need extra strength.

The rain had stopped. "It's getting dark," observed

Amelia as she got out the galvanized washtub. "Time for all niños to have their baths and go to bed."

Julia, who was ten and almost a woman, helped her mother bring buckets of water from the well. Soon all three children, shiny-clean and smelling of soap, had snuggled into their sarapes and were sound asleep.

Amelia said, "You'd better get some sleep too, Paco. I'll wake you when it's time to go for the shovel."

Paco was tired after his day's work. Obediently, he wrapped himself in his sarape and lay down on the sleeping mat. "I'll rest," he said, "but I'm too worried to sleep."

The next thing he knew, Amelia was shaking him. "Wake up," she whispered, "it's time. I'm coming with you."

Silently, Paco got to his feet and walked out into the chilly night. He saw Amelia throw an old sarape around her shoulders. She stepped to his side, and together they padded down the dark lane to the house of Don Porfirio. Paco found the magic shovel leaning against the gate.

It was the time of night when all good people were at home in their beds, for everyone knew that evil spirits walked abroad in the darkest hours. Paco and Amelia stumbled through the blackness, holding hands like frightened children. Looming shadows seemed to follow them, transforming familiar objects into grotesque shapes. They found their way with little trouble only because Paco had walked this same path a thousand times in daylight.

A three-quarter moon hung close to the horizon, providing just enough light for Paco to find the row of corn where he'd discovered the body that morning. However, as soon as they entered the cornfield, even this small source of illumination was cut off. Here between the rows, it was so dark that Paco had to feel his way.

The air was heavy with the odor of wet foliage. He listened closely for night sounds, but all he could hear was his own breathing and the rustle of cornstalks whenever the wind stirred. Amelia crept close behind him, one hand clutching his shirt between his shoulder blades. The pressure of that small fist against his back lent Paco immeasurable comfort.

When Paco's bare foot struck the first broken stalk lying across the row, he stopped and bent down to locate the body with his hands. It had the smell of death about it now and its clothes were sopping wet from the afternoon rain. He hated to touch it.

"All day I've been trying to decide where to dig the grave," he whispered to Amelia. "There isn't room between the rows, and I don't want to destroy any of the corn. Besides, with all this rain, the water table is very close to the surface. I'm afraid that if I dig a deep hole, it will fill with water and the corpse will float."

"That's why I brought this old sarape," murmured Amelia. "We can use it to carry the body out of the corn patch onto higher ground."

"*Qué bueno!*" said Paco. He could always count on Amelia. "We'll drag him up the hill and plant him where no crops are growing."

The body was heavy and ungainly, nearly impossible to control in the dark. The arms and legs flopped as if the man were deliberately clutching at corn stalks to impede his own removal. By the time Paco and Amelia managed to extricate his limbs from between the stalks and roll his soggy corpse onto the sarape, they were panting and in a state of near terror.

"I'll pull," whispered Paco, "and you guide him from behind. Voices carry a long way at night, so don't speak unless you have to." He grunted and heaved, the body slid. Amelia staggered along behind, holding up the two rear corners of the sarape. Paco could tell from the way his burden yawed that she lifted the sides alternately, rolling the corpse just enough to keep it from slipping off into the mud. They seemed to move in an endless black void, but after a long time they came to the end of the row and burst out into fresh air and moonlight.

Paco straightened his back and wiped the sweat out of

his eyes. There was no time for rest. On they went, groaning, dragging the heavy load past the cork oak tree, around an organ cactus and uphill to an open spot.

Paco set to work.

Down where the corn was planted, the earth was soft and damp. Up here on the hillside, the soil was rocky and the rain had run off without sinking into the ground. Over and over, Paco had to strike with the shovel, straining to find a spot where he could drive it into the earth. Amelia dropped to her knees and grubbed with both hands to pull stones out of the way.

A couple of feet down, the rocks thinned out and the digging went more smoothly. Paco remembered that Don Porfirio had said to bury the body deep, so he jumped into the hole and kept digging until he could no longer see over the sides. It took a long time and he grew very tired.

At last he cut a couple of footholds and laid the shovel across the top of the hole. By the time he had struggled out of the grave, he had to rest. He flopped on his back beside the corpse.

"In the name of all that's holy," he whispered to himself, "what am I doing here?" He was so weary and so thoroughly sickened by the smell of the body next to him that he had almost forgotten his fear.

Amelia, practical as always, forced herself with obvious reluctance to pat the soggy pockets of the dead man. "Empty," she murmured in a relieved whisper. "Should we wrap him in the sarape before we put him into the grave?"

"No!" whispered Paco. "Don't waste a sarape on him! We'll just dump him in and cover him up."

But when the grave was filled, they were faced with a new problem; what to do with the rocks they had unearthed during the digging. If they piled them on the grave, it would look like a grave and that would cause questions. Paco stood there in the feeble moonlight and raised his arms in an exaggerated, hopeless shrug. Where could they put these stupid rocks?

"Let's disguise the grave," suggested Amelia. "Then we can pile the leftover dirt and rocks on the sarape, pull them around to the other side of the hill and scatter them."

Paco glanced at the sky, then nodded agreement. During the hours he'd been digging, the moon had crept overhead. It hung there, pale and lopsided, seeming to mock them, grudging them enough chill light to do their work.

First they trampled and jumped on the surface of the grave to pack it down. Then Amelia found a branch, and Paco used it to scratch the soil and remove their footprints. They scattered small rocks over the grave, spreading them unevenly and pressing them into the earth.

By the time they had dragged the bigger rocks to the other side of the hill, Paco was so exasperated that he dumped them unceremoniously and let them roll where they would. He shook the sarape until it snapped and dirt flew in all directions. "I've had more than enough of this," he whispered fiercely. "Let's go home."

"We have to return the shovel," Amelia reminded him, "and have all this erased from our memories."

Paco was so tired that his bones ached and his muscles quivered. All he wanted was to go home and sleep for the few hours left to him this night. But by the time they had stumbled back to the village, he agreed that it would be sensible to return the shovel and carry out the rest of the brujo's orders.

Don Porfirio was waiting for them by candlelight. As always, the old man's behavior was pompous, his expression stern. The ceremony was brief, perhaps because of the hour. He muttered incantations as he put nails on their heads, and he had them drink from a gourd filled with *chichicaxtle*, the herb that erased memory.

At last they headed for home. By the time they got to bed, it was almost time to get up. Like it or not, Paco knew he'd have to go to work as usual or his neighbors would wonder what was wrong.

They struggled through breakfast. Julia and the boys got ready for school. Paco felt dull and exhausted, as if he were moving in a bad dream.

His father nudged him. "How did it go last night?" he asked eagerly. "What happened?"

"How should I know?" snapped Paco. "My memory has been erased."

Amelia handed him his lunch without her customary smile. Paco took his wooden hoe and shuffled through the village and out into the countryside. His head felt hot and he wondered despairingly if God had put a curse on him for being proud of his corn.

Then he felt the cool dust squish between his toes and he heard the little doves coo, and he had to smile. He felt much better; still exhausted, but hopeful. He went directly to the row where he had found the body and walked along it with confidence. Today he would hoe beyond that fatal spot and finish his job.

The three cornstalks were still there. Almost exuberantly Paco picked them up in his arms and tossed them aside.

And there—*Madre de Dios!* There was another body! He nearly screamed. A hasty glance told him that this one, too, had a hole between his eyes and a trickle of dried blood. But this was not a rich man. This one was dressed in the everyday grubby clothing of a *campesino*, a farmer. He was very young and his face wore an expression of great sadness. *Pobrecito!*

With a sob of fear, Paco threw down his hoe and spun around. He dug his toes into the mud and sprang forward, running for home, head down, arms pumping. He had taken only a few strides toward the safety of the village when he felt himself lifted straight up into the air and clasped to a broad chest by a pair of huge, fleshy arms. Hot breath seared his forehead. His arms flailed, he tried to turn aside, couldn't, smelled garlic, sweat, saw only a wide expanse of plaid shirt. He struggled valiantly, kicking out like a burro with heel flies, but he might have been battling the air itself for all the effect it had. His exertions gradually subsided until, helpless and humiliated, he hung like a rag doll in the giant's grasp.

The moment he was still, Paco felt himself lowered to his feet. Staggering backward, he looked up into the glittering eyes of an immense man with a curling, black beard; a *gigante*, very tall and enormously wide, who had materialized as if by magic to stand in the middle of the row and lift Paco in his great arms.

"*Con cuidado*, Paquito," the huge man said, with a deep chuckle. "Go softly, my little friend, for you and I are partners. We'll be farming together from now on."

CHAPTER 2

Paco's heart labored so hard that he thought it might jump out of his chest. He stared at the ground and struggled to contain his panic. Try as he might, he could not squeeze his thoughts into logical order; they dipped and swirled like frantic bats at dusk.

Partners? At least the answer to that was clear enough: *Ni de loco!* Not even if I were crazy!

On the edge of his vision were the big man's enormous feet. Gradually Paco's attention riveted on them in dreadful fascination. Those feet were clad in high, white leather athletic shoes with thick, gray soles and purple shoe laces. They were the most colossal footwear Paco had ever seen. Each shoe was easily the size of Don Porfirio's shovel. Paco found himself spellbound by those shoes, and the distraction helped him control his fear and anger.

With great effort, he slid his gaze away to examine the face of the dead campesino one more time. He wanted to make sure that he didn't know the poor fellow.

The big man looked down at the body too, chuckling companionably. "Just look at that, Paquito," he said, "I'm afraid you have another corpse to dispose of."

Paco felt a burst of almost uncontrollable rage. "No

thank you, señor," he said, his voice polite but firm. "I did the other one. This one's yours."

"Ah, but it's your cornfield, Paquito."

"Sí, señor," Paco said, drawing himself up to his full five-feet-three-inches. "It is my cornfield, but it is your corpse." He gulped then, taken aback by his own boldness.

Even as he warned himself to be careful, he felt reckless outrage swelling within his breast at being called "Paquito," Little Paco, repeatedly. The word should be loving and personal; his family had called him Paquito when he was a small child. In the mouth of El Gigante it was demeaning. It's a mere word, he soothed himself, so put down the stick, Paco: only a stupid man jabs a stick at a rabid dog.

Amelia often teased him, saying that his face was so open that thoughts slid across it in procession for all the world to see. He struggled now to appear impassive. Bravely, he fought to develop instant guile, knowing that defiance would bring only disaster. At the same time, he made a private and stubborn pledge to himself: he would not spend another night out here, surrounded by evil spirits, digging a grave in the moonlight.

Armored with what he hoped was an air of innocence, Paco looked up into the face of the big stranger. The man's full lips curved in a benevolent smile, but his eyes were a serpent's eyes, glittering and cold. Paco barely suppressed a shudder. He asked urgently, "Where did these dead men come from, señor? Who are they?"

"Dear Paquito," the man said with false gentleness, "they are my *former* partners."

Paco caught his breath. *Ay, caramba!* this was like the time he got mired in quicksand down by the river. The more he struggled, the worse things got. "I think you must have mistaken me for someone else, señor," he said with only a slight quaver in his voice. "I have little to bring to any partnership."

"The land, Paquito! I need your land and your knowledge of farming to grow a special crop for me."

"I would be glad to share my special corn crop w̄ señor, if you were needy. You do not seem to be a poor ˌ yet you are asking me to take food out of my childre. mouths and share it with you. This I cannot do."

The giant threw back his head and laughed. Paco waited. Surprised. Wary.

"I don't want your corn, Paquito, I have other seeds for you to sow. In between the cornstalks of your next crop, tall, strong marijuana plants will thrive. With my magic seeds and your skill at growing things, we will make a fortune."

So that was it! Everyone had heard of local farmers who'd been forced to grow marijuana for Mexico City gangsters like this one. The campesinos had to give up their precious corn, their food for the coming year, to make room for marijuana plants. Somehow, their share of the profits was never enough to make up for the loss of the corn, never enough to buy food for their families. Even worse, if federales found the plants, it was the farmer who went to jail while the gangsters went free. Paco had heard that these bad men offered only two alternatives to a farmer: cooperation or death.

Involuntarily, Paco's glance flickered toward the dead campesino. Clearly, this young farmer had made the wrong choice.

Paco faced El Gigante squarely, tipped his head back and gazed into the terrible cold eyes. He was so frightened that he felt weak and the back of his neck ached. He knew that he'd never be able to think clearly until he got far away from the smothering presence of this huge man.

Taking a deep breath, Paco forced his expression to remain dignified, impassive. He said, "*Con permiso*, señor. If you'll excuse me, I have much work to do."

Slowly he turned his back on the giant. Knees trembling, expecting a bullet to smack between his shoulder blades at any moment, he stepped over the dead campesino, picked up his hoe and began to till the corn. Sweating, terrified, on down the long row he moved, not stopping until he reached the far side of the field. As he hoed around the last plant, a peal of distant, raucous laughter made him jump. When he whirled to look back, no one was there. The big man had vanished. For good? Somehow, Paco didn't think so.

Work was the only way he knew to curb his fear. He toiled up one row and down the next, stubbornly ignoring the corpse of the campesino. Like a mechanical man he dragged his hoe from one cornstalk to the next and as he worked, he tried to muddle through his problems. He'd been freed from the immediate presence of the giant, so he should be able to think, but he was so weary from last night's exertions that his thoughts merely squirmed like horned toads settling into the dust.

Lunchtime came. Paco munched his tortillas and went on working. An hour later he was staggering from fatigue. He knew that he must either go home for a nap or lie down right here in the middle of his cornfield. At any other time the idea of a siesta among the corn stalks would have been appealing, but today it seemed dangerous. Not only was there a dead body and its restless ghost a few yards away, but the gigantic stranger could reappear at any moment. Paco wanted to be awake and on his feet if that should happen.

At last, in sheer desperation he left off in the middle of a row and headed for home. If the neighbors snickered and called him lazy behind his back, it couldn't be helped. He simply had to get some sleep and he didn't dare to shut his eyes until he was secure in his own home with his family close around him.

The gate was ajar. Paco stumbled through it, past his father and Amelia, and went directly into the house. In a daze he unrolled his sleeping mat, wrapped himself in his sarape and lay down with a groan of relief. He fell into profound, instant slumber.

Amelia woke him for supper. He chewed and swallowed automatically, tasting nothing.

Grandfather joked with the children, as usual. Paco,

sick with dread, took Tonio, the youngest, onto his lap and put his arms around him protectively. He watched Juan and Julia with tender, loving eyes, feeling crushed by the immensity of his responsibilities and his love for his family.

"What did you do at school today?" asked Grandfather.

"We played soccer," said Tonio, wriggling excitedly on Paco's lap, "and our team won!"

Juan, the older brother, said with pompous scorn, "Soccer is fun, but it's not very important. Books are important." He turned to his grandfather. "Today we read one of the stories about the rabbit and the coyote."

"I like those stories," said Julia.

"So do I," said Juan. "The coyote is big and strong. He could eat the poor little rabbit any time, but the rabbit always outsmarts him and gets away."

"The old Zapotec stories are still the best," said Grandfather, smiling.

Paco shivered. In the presence of the giant, his mind had been as paralyzed as a frightened rabbit cornered by a coyote. Now, here by his own fire, his reasoning powers began to stir at last, like the rich earth curling slowly under the plow. Could he learn from those old tales, he wondered. Could he, the miserable rabbit, possibly humble the coyote? He felt a faint quiver of hope.

Paco returned to his bed. His eyes fell shut. As he hovered briefly on the edge of sleep Amelia's soft voice penetrated his consciousness.

"Julia and I have finished weaving that large order of place mats for Doña Milly at Casa Colonial," she said. "Can you go to Oaxaca with me tomorrow morning when I deliver them to her? I thought we could catch the early bus."

Paco found it impossible to open his sleep-filled eyes, but he managed a smile and a happy nod. If he didn't go to his cornfield tomorrow, he'd have one more whole day to think over the unreasonable demands of El Gigante. Perhaps, thought Paco, given enough time, he could figure a way out of this terrible mess.

CHAPTER 3

Doña Milly sat on one of the Victorian sofas in the *sala* of her Casa Colonial, a large thick book open across her lap. Her stiff old fingers crept over the pages sideways like small hesitant crabs. She sat primly, back straight, ankles crossed, eyes tightly closed. Her white curls quivered as she bent her neck in earnest concentration.

When her fingers repeated a word twice, then stumbled to a halt, she snorted in vexation and her eyes flew open. "Reading Braille," she muttered, "is the absolute shits!"

For someone who'd always been a rapid, voracious reader until she lost much of her sight at age fifty-two, learning to make slow sense of those minuscule bumps had been an agony of frustration. The peripheral vision she'd retained didn't seem to help at all.

"This might as well be in some foreign language," she had complained to Herbert one day long ago. "It feels like the damned page has a rash."

"Maybe it's written in German measles," he'd suggested, chuckling merrily at his own wit.

At the time Milly hadn't found her husband's remark at all funny. Now she could smile about it, but it was far too late to share the joke with Herbert. She still missed him terribly, sometimes with a deep, futile anger at being left behind, all alone, to cope with the various problems of their little hotel. Refusing to brood about it, she bent forward and explored the bumps on the page once again.

Many years ago, when her fingers had been more nimble, she had attacked Braille with stubborn persistence. Eventually she had triumphed. Nowadays, thank God, talking books arrived once a month from Washington, D.C. Even so, she practiced Braille frequently, telling herself that a skill so hard-won should not be allowed to merely slip away.

She owned just one book in Braille, *The House of Exile* by Nora Waln. She thought the title apt for an expatriate like herself, for no matter how much she had enjoyed these past few years here in Oaxaca, she still thought of Iowa as "home."

When Milly heard the big front door of The Casa open she knew that Inocencio, her manager, had arrived for the day. She slammed the book, shoved it into its customary place between the cushion and the arm of the sofa, and put a pillow over it. Then she headed for Inocencio's office out in the large entryway. She had a bone to pick with him.

Her own Casa was familiar and unchanging, so she moved at her usual brisk trot down the forty-foot length of the sala, past the other sofa, a game table, various easy chairs, the library table and benches, and the fireplace. She stepped onto the veranda that encircled the patio, took nine quick steps to the left, turned left again and dropped into the leather chair beside Inocencio's big desk.

"Good morning," she said.

"Good morning, Doña Milly. How are you today?"

"Fine, thank you, Inocencio. I know you're busy, so I'll get right to the point. I found a hole in my bath towel this morning. We must need new towels, right?"

"Yes, I've been meaning to talk to you about that."

"When you have time will you please count all the good towels so we'll know how many new ones to order?"

"I've already done that, señora. There are forty-nine face towels and fifty-two bath towels, but thirty-six of the bath towels have holes in them. I suggest that we replace them sometime soon."

Sometime soon? It was shocking to think of thirty-six holey towels finding their way into the thirteen bathrooms of Casa Colonial. What must her guests think?

Inocencio said, "I thought we should order thirty-six new towels and make washcloths out of the old ones with the holes in them. It would be a shame to waste the parts of those old towels that are still perfectly good."

Milly knew that Inocencio hated to spend money; even her money. She'd try a compromise. "That's fine. Make the washcloths. But we need more than thirty-six new towels. Please buy enough so that we have three sets for each bathroom. And be sure to get the very best quality."

"Señora," groaned Inocencio, "we do not need so many towels. It is a waste of—"

Milly frowned and held up one hand. "Just a moment," she said. "Listen!"

Out in the patio some man was talking to Elpidio, the young gardener, in a voice that Milly could only think of as a cigar-smoker's gargle. Elpidio was mellow and courteous, but clearly upset. The conversation broke off abruptly and Elpidio's footsteps came hurrying toward her. As he drew near, he broke into voluble and aggrieved Spanish.

Milly leaned forward to give him her full attention. She and Herbert had learned the language, mostly from books, just before they'd left Iowa. She knew her Spanish was simple and stilted. No matter. Elpidio was Zapotec, so Spanish was his second language too. They understood each other.

"*Patrona*," Elpidio said, his voice quivering, "I'm sure your conference with Don Inocencio is very, very important. I hope you'll forgive me for interrupting."

"Certainly, Elpidio, you're forgiven. What's wrong?"

"I'm having trouble with one of the guests, patrona. He

follows me around the garden, telling me how to do my work. Yesterday he instructed me in pruning the *bugambilla*. That was fine, I'm perfectly willing to learn. But today he asked me if I have ever grown marijuana here at Casa Colonial. Marijuana is illegal, patrona. I am insulted by his question."

"Maybe he's bored, Elpidio. I suggest that you pay no attention to him."

"May I respectfully remind you, patrona, that you told me to be courteous to the guests, so I cannot just turn my back on him."

"That is true, Elpidio. But now I give you permission to say, 'Please excuse me, señor, but I must get on with my work.' And then you walk away."

"Gracias, señora. But if he persists, what then?"

"Then you send him to me and I'll scold him as if he's a naughty little boy."

Elpidio laughed.

"I know who he's talking about," said Inocencio in English. "Señor Rodolfo Sánchez from Mexico City. He and his wife and daughter are staying in rooms seven and eight."

"Oh, yes," said Milly. "I talked with the wife and daughter at breakfast this morning. They're quite charming. But I haven't met the husband yet."

"That's because he ordered me to send all his meals to his room. It's a lot of trouble, but I guess we'll have to do it." Inocencio's voice dropped to a confidential murmur. "They are a rather strange family. The daughter is near thirty, I'd say, but she is not married."

"I wonder why not."

"I don't know. She's quite good-looking, but the parents are over-protective. They treat that young woman as if she's a little child. The mother and daughter are always together. They come and go like most tourists, but the father never joins them. And he wears dark glasses all the time, even indoors."

"Perhaps he has problems with his vision."

"I don't think so. When they first checked in, he asked for a key to the front door."

"Don't give him one," ordered Milly. "He can ring the doorbell like all the other guests."

"I agree. I told him there are no extra keys. Half an hour later he asked me about that old door in the outside wall of the vacant lot."

"Our vacant lot?"

"Yes, the one that's part of this property. I told him there is no key to that little door and that it is never opened because the lock and hinges are rusted."

"Is that true?"

"Yes, it's true."

"And did he accept this?"

"Oh, yes. In fact, he seemed quite happy about it. As far as I can tell, he hasn't left the house since they got here. He's an odd one, señora. I'm watching him closely."

"Good for you! I wonder if he's a narcotics agent or something. It was preposterous for him to ask Elpidio if we grow marijuana here."

Elpidio, who did not speak English, jumped back into the conversation when he heard the word "marijuana." "Not only is it illegal, patrona," he pronounced loftily, "but it would be especially foolish to plant marijuana here inside the walls of Casa Colonial for all the guests to see. The appearance of marijuana leaves is unmistakable, you know, and when the plant blooms it has a distinctive odor."

Milly wondered how he knew so much about it. She thought it best not to ask.

The doorbell rang. Elpidio went back to his gardening and Inocencio crossed the entryway to throw open the front door.

Milly glimpsed a huge figure silhouetted against the bright sunlight reflecting off the street. Even with her distorted vision she could tell that this man filled the entire doorway. He stepped over the threshold without waiting to be invited and slammed the door behind him.

Milly jumped at the sound.

"I want Señor Rodolfo Sánchez, and I want him now!" the newcomer announced in rumbling Spanish. "Bring him to me at once."

Milly's hackles rose. This fellow must be from somewhere near the U.S. border where, she'd heard, people were always rude to each other. She frowned and drew herself up, ready to tell the great lummox to mind his manners.

Before she could say a word, Inocencio spoke in a voice dripping with deference. "Honored sir, I don't know anyone called Rodolfo Sánchez."

Milly opened her mouth to correct him, then shut it again as Herbert's voice spoke clearly, somewhere inside her mind. *Hush, Mildred!* he told her. *Wait and see.*

Milly gave a quick little nod and subsided.

The big man growled, "If Sánchez isn't here now, he'll be coming soon. I'll wait." And he strode out into the garden.

As if he *owns* the place, Milly thought angrily. She felt Inocencio take her hand and she looked up, startled. "Señora, let me show you where the sala is," Inocencio said, as if she were a new guest in the hotel and a total stranger.

"Thank you, señor," said Milly, playing along. She permitted herself to be led down the veranda, into the sala, and over to the sofa at the far end of the room.

"Now!" she whispered. "What the hell is going on? Why did you lie about knowing Rodolfo Sánchez?"

"Because I don't trust that big man."

"Why not?"

"For one thing, he smiles all the time, but his eyes look as mean as a snake's. He's dangerous—a big city criminal, señora. I'm sure of it."

Milly usually accepted Inocencio's assessments of people, especially Mexicans, without question, but this time she was taken aback. "A criminal, Inocencio? How can you possibly tell that just by looking at him?"

"Not just by looking at him, but also by listening to how

he talks. He's obviously uneducated, yet I can tell that he doesn't work for a living because his hands are clean and soft."

"I agree that he's a rude clod, but soft hands don't necessarily make him a criminal."

"Yes, but he's wearing a gold Rolex watch and a lot of gold chains around his neck, and a pair of those two-hundred-dollar American athletic shoes. Where did he get the money to buy all that stuff? Not by selling tortillas! And then he almost knocked me over when he went into the patio. Anyone that crude and with so much money has to be a criminal. At least that's what I think."

Milly nodded. "You could be right," she said. "You'd better find Rodolfo Sánchez and have him get this fellow out of here."

"I plan to do that, señora, but first I wanted to protect you; to bring you into the sala and as far away from that man as possible. If he's a Mexico City mobster, as I suspect, we must not let him know that you own this casa. I'll feel much more comfortable if you are anomalous."

"That's 'anonymous,'" said Milly, "and stop fussing over me as if I'm some fuddy-duddy." Nevertheless, she was pleased and quite touched to be so cared for. She heard Inocencio's brisk footsteps whisper across the oriental rug as he headed for the door. Halfway there he paused and came back again.

"What's the matter?" she asked.

"He's in the hammock. I can see him through the window."

"Who, Sánchez?"

"No! That big thug is in our hammock. He has pulled up the sides to cover himself completely. He looks like a fat caterpillar in a cocoon."

A caterpillar? Milly shuddered. "Inocencio, please find Rodolfo Sánchez! Have him get rid of this man as soon as he possibly can."

As Inocencio went out the door, Milly sat down, got

out her book, and laid it across her knees. But she didn't even try to read. All her senses were focused on waiting for Inocencio's return.

In a few minutes he came back into the room and eased onto the sofa beside her.

"Sánchez has disappeared," he said quietly. "He was here half an hour ago bothering Elpidio, but now I can't find him anywhere."

Inocencio went over to stand by the window. He said, "That man is so heavy that the hammock is almost touching the ground. I'm afraid it's going to break."

"I hope it does!" snapped Milly. "If he falls on his big behind, maybe he'll leave. Keep looking for Sánchez, Inocencio, he must be here inside our walls somewhere."

How frustrating it was to have to sit here waiting. She wished she could search out Sánchez for herself and insist that he get rid of the fat caterpillar in the hammock.

Before Inocencio could leave the room, the doorbell rang again. "Goodness!" Milly complained. "This place is as busy as a cantina on Saturday night."

Inocencio left to answer the door, returning almost immediately to announce in Spanish, "Here are Paco and Amelia from Santo Tomás Jalieza, Doña Milly." In English he added, "I'll wait in the office where I can keep an eye on you-know-who in the hammock."

Oh, dear. This was hardly the most convenient time for Paco and Amelia to have arrived, thought Milly. But she put that out of her mind as she walked the length of the room, hands outstretched to welcome her visitors.

"Buenos días, amigos," she said.

"Buenos días, Doña Milly," chorused Amelia amd Paco.

Amelia said, "I have the twenty-four yellow place mats you ordered for your table, señora. Would you like to look at them?"

The moment she heard Amelia's gentle voice, Milly's heart grew calm. These dear people were like an island of serenity in her muddled morning. Contentedly, she asked about Paco's father and the children while Paco took the new place mats out of a white plastic sack and stacked them on the library table.

Milly smiled as she caught a glimpse of yellow. "Your placemats are like golden sunshine," she said, running her hands over the pile. "Exactly what I wanted. Did you happen to bring any other things with you, Amelia?"

"I brought a matching yellow runner for the center of the table, señora, and I have another set of mats in blue, in case you're interested. And here is—"

"Momentito, Amelia," Paco interrupted, his voice tense. He had moved over by the window. "There is a man in your hammock, Doña Milly. I can see his enormous feet sticking out. He's wearing white shoes with purple shoelaces."

Purple shoelaces? Milly giggled. Oddly, Paco sounded as if he were upset.

"Yes, Paco," she soothed, "he has big feet because he is a very large man."

"Is he staying at Casa Colonial, señora?"

Paco spoke quietly in the manner of a proper Zapotec. His words were slow and without emphasis, but Milly detected enormous stress underlying his question.

"No, he says he's waiting for one of our guests. Paco, do you know this man?"

"I hope not, señora. But yesterday I did meet someone wearing shoes exactly like the ones hanging out of your hammock. Amelia," he urged suddenly, "never mind the runner. We really must go." He hurried over to the table and began to cram Amelia's weavings back into the sack.

"Please stay just a little longer," Milly pleaded. "I do want the yellow mats and the runner and also the blue placemats, and I'd like to see the other things you brought."

Milly noticed that Paco held his breath for a long moment before letting it out again. Are you all right?" she asked. "Can I get you a *refresco*, Paco? A cup of coffee, perhaps?"

"No, thank you, señora. It's just that I thought of something I need to do at home and so we must hurry."

Milly heard great fear in his voice. He was trying to be polite, but seemed to grow ever more frantic as she and Amelia took the rest of the weavings out of the sack and examined them.

Amelia explained, "We are a little bit nervous today, señora, because the federales arrived at our village just as we were getting on the bus to come here. We are worried about the children and the grandfather."

"What's it all about, Amelia?"

"We don't know yet, señora. The federales wouldn't tell us."

Hastily, Paco repacked the few items Milly rejected. Then, leaving the things she was buying stacked on the table, he snatched up the sack and almost dragged Amelia out the door. Milly followed them to Inocencio's desk where they stopped just long enough to collect their money.

Paco whispered, "Adiós, Doña Milly, y muchas gracias." Then he hustled Amelia out into the street.

Milly stood by Inocencio's desk, staring after them. "What a crazy morning this has been," she said. "Even easy, familiar things are slipping out of kilter. Amelia says there are federales at Santo Tomás Jalieza today. I wonder why. Keep your ears open for gossip, Inocencio."

There was a sudden loud crack and an earth-shaking thud from the patio. Milly whirled toward the sound. Inocencio jumped to his feet.

"Your stupid hammock broke and dropped me on the ground," shouted the big man. "I'm tired of waiting, anyway." He moved swiftly into the office, brushing past Milly as if she didn't exist. He stopped in front of Inocencio and spoke in a menacing sneer. "*Hombrecito*, little man, you tell that stinking Rodolfo Sánchez that I'll be back. Soon!"

"I still don't know any Sánchez, but if he comes, I'll tell him. What name shall I give him, señor?" Inocencio asked with brave courtesy.

The big man gave a hoarse chuckle that bubbled nastily in his throat. It was not a pleasant sound. "My name is *El Diablo!*" he said with lingering venom. "Tell him the devil was here."

Milly gasped and backed up a step, repelled and a bit frightened by his voice and manner. She edged closer to Inocencio, and they huddled there in flabbergasted silence as the man who called himself El Diablo stepped out into the street and slammed the door behind him.

"Whew!" said Milly. She backed up to the leather chair, feeling for it with one trembling hand. Her knees buckled and she sat down hard. She blinked several times and tried to collect herself.

She heard Inocencio stumble over the feet of his swivel chair as he plunked himself into it. He opened and closed the top drawer of his desk a couple of times as if he were acting busy while he gathered his wits. He swiveled his chair back and forth. Milly could hear it squeal and the sound set her teeth on edge. Poor Inocencio was more agitated than she had ever known him to be.

In an effort to break the tension, Milly leaned forward and glared at him in mock ferocity, then rapped on the desk with her knuckles. She lowered her voice as far as it would go. "And now, hombrecito," she growled, "about those bath towels with the holes in them..."

Inocencio burst into a peal of high-pitched laughter, sounding immensely relieved.

Milly grinned and stood up. Her knees were still wobbly. She said, "When Rodolfo Sánchez finally shows up, please ask him to keep that big man out of here. He's clearly a menace and I don't want him around."

"All right, señora, I'll tell Sánchez. I hope it works."

Milly headed through the orchid arbor at her usual brisk pace and turned down the path through the garden, longing for the sanctuary of her cottage. When she came to the laundry room she peered in through the open door.

"Ramona?" she called in Spanish. "May I have a clean towel, please?"

Someone coughed and there was a rustling sound over in the corner behind the washing machine, but Ramona didn't answer. Jesus! Now what?

There was a definite reek of stale cigar overriding the everyday, comfortable aroma of hot water and soapsuds. Milly fumbled for the light switch and flicked it on, then cleared her throat, searching for the school-teacher voice she seldom used these days. "Who's in here?" she demanded. "Answer me!"

"Ramona is not here, señora," a man replied in a cigar-smoker's gargle. "I'm looking for her, too."

You are not! Milly thought wrathfully. You're Rodolfo Sánchez, you're hiding from the giant who wears purple shoelaces, and I'm damned well going to find out why!

CHAPTER 4

Milly knew that most Mexican men would be too proud to skulk in a laundry room, a work area strictly for women. Surely Rodolfo Sánchez had heard the big man leave, yet here he was, still cowering behind her old-fashioned wringer washing machine, puffing his smelly cigar.

She could forgive Sánchez for wanting to hide, but she could not forgive him for leaving her to face that terrible big man with nobody to back her up but Inocencio. Sánchez had sucked the two of them right into the midst of his problems, whatever they were. It was decidedly unfair.

In her mind she heard Herbert's voice say, *Mildred, you are responsible for Casa Colonial, your employees, and all your guests. So find out what's going on.*

Damned right, I will! she pledged silently.

Milly straightened her spine and trotted out her most careful Spanish. "You must be Rodolfo Sánchez," she said sweetly, easing into the cover of her gracious-hostess persona. It was a role she had perfected through eight years of dealing with all sorts of guests. "I'm Doña Milly, the dueña of Casa Colonial." She extended a cordial hand and waited.

The cigar smell grew even stronger as Sánchez edged

around the washing machine and moved toward her. He responded with a handshake so fleeting that Milly barely had time to notice that the pad at the base of his thumb was soft and fleshy. His grip was gentle, almost feminine. This is the hand of a sensualist, she thought in surprise, and he may act smooth, but he's not very sure of himself. Or maybe he's suspicious of everyone.

That's silly, whispered Herbert's voice inside her head. *You can't judge character by the feel of a person's hand.*

Well, I know that, she snapped. *But sometimes, like now, it's all I have to go on.*

Aloud she said to Sánchez, "If you're looking for Ramona, she is probably in the kitchen. Shall I call her for you, señor?"

"Thank you for your concern, Doña Milly, but that is not necessary. I'll find her later."

"Muy bien, señor. By the way, I wish to tell you that I met your lovely wife and daughter at breakfast this morning. Your daughter Yolanda is a charming young woman and quite beautiful."

"Thank you, señora. Your kind words cause my paternal heart to swell with pride. Yolanda is our most precious jewel. Her mother and I thank God for her every day of our lives."

My goodness but Sánchez was suave; what her Aunt Marie used to call A Real Classy Gent. His accent was impeccable and his words flowed with a syrupy elegance that contrasted oddly with his rough, smoker's voice. For an instant Milly was embarrassed by her own awkward Spanish and childish vocabulary. Stubbornly, she decided to employ her seeming naivete to disarm this polished gentleman.

"Have you seen our garden?" she asked with a delicate smile and a fluttery little gesture toward the flower beds. "Our guests are welcome to explore everywhere, you know." She moved slowly down the path and Sánchez fell into step beside her. She kept up a light chatter while she searched her mind for a way to ask questions about the big man in the hammock. Was Sánchez employing this same time to marshal his defenses? she wondered. Would their conversation proceed like a fencing match?

"This property was once a private home," she began. "When my husband and I took it over, it had just five bedrooms and three bathrooms. We modernized the old kitchen and I have added ten more bedrooms and bathrooms over the years."

"It is a beautiful house, señora, and quite perfect in every way. Obviously, your husband is a businesslike and efficient man."

Milly pretended confusion. "You knew my late husband? Oh!" she giggled, "you're thinking of Inocencio. I am a widow, señor, and Inocencio is my employee. He is the manager of Casa Colonial and he is definitely married to someone else! Inocencio and his Lidia have thirteen children and forty-eight grandchildren, all fine, productive citizens. A remarkable achievement, verdad?"

"Remarkable indeed, señora, especially in these parlous times. Nowadays many young people eschew the values taught by those of us who are older and wiser."

To Milly, his voice sounded long-suffering, as if he spoke from bitter experience, yet she had sensed no rebellion in his daughter. Interesting.

"I always have coffee on the veranda at this hour," she said. "Will you join me?"

"Thank you, señora, coffee would be very welcome."

They stopped at a round leather table outside rooms seven and eight where the Sánchez family were staying. Sánchez held Milly's chair with a courtly flourish, then seated himself across from her.

While she waited for Graciela to spot them and bring their coffee, Milly's thoughts flew, seeking a graceful approach to the subject foremost in her mind; the huge man who'd demanded an audience with Rodolfo Sánchez. Finally, she gave an inward sigh and waded right in, relying on her little-old-lady persona to soften the bluntness.

"I suppose you know that a man came looking for you earlier this morning." She heard the leather chair creak as Sánchez shifted his weight. He did not answer. "The man was extremely large and aggressive. He called himself The Devil, but I can't imagine that El Diablo was his true name. I think you must know who he is, señor."

Silence.

"Inocencio couldn't find you, so we assumed that you didn't wish to talk with the fellow."

"You are perceptive, señora," Sánchez said drily. "It is true that I avoided the man and will continue to do so. I am on vacation and refuse to be disturbed."

But you didn't care how much he disturbed me! thought Milly with a flash of anger.

She managed to cover her resentment with a motherly smile. "Don't worry, my friend," she murmured, "Inocencio told the fellow that we'd never heard of you. Perhaps he won't come back."

Sánchez laughed. "I sincerely hope not, señora."

"I hope not, too, señor, because frankly, I'm afraid of him. Would you mind telling me how you happen to be connected with such a person? I ask only because I have concern for the safety of my house and the reputation of my business."

"I understand completely, señora. You must realize that I did not see the man today. But based on the sound of his voice alone, I don't recall ever having known him."

There had been a subtle change in the timbre of the rasping voice. It had moved half a notch lower and had become even more lubricious. It was clear to Milly that Sánchez had just told an adroit and buttery lie. He knew the man!

She kept probing. "It would be hard to forget this fellow if you had ever met him. He is so big that he completely fills a doorway. He has enormous feet, a deep voice, and a curly black beard, according to Inocencio."

"I must admit, señora, that your description reminds me

strongly of a business partner I had at one time. But once I retired and dissolved the company, there was no longer a connection between us. Let us hope that you will never see this man again, whoever he is."

"Yes, let us hope!"

She smiled confidingly. "I'll tell you something amusing about your perhaps-former partner. He climbed into the hammock while he waited for you, and it broke. When he landed on the ground we thought it was an earthquake." She leaned forward for dramatic effect. "I hope his big fat bottom hurts a lot. It would serve him right for acting so unpleasant."

Rodolfo Sánchez produced a deep chuckle which became a wheeze which turned into a prolonged coughing spell. "Thank you for that wonderful image, señora," he gurgled. "I'll treasure it until the day I die!"

Which may be quite soon, if you don't lay off the cigars! thought Milly.

Just as the clock on the faraway Basílica de Soledad chimed eleven-forty-five Graciela arrived with a tray. A moment later, the doorbell rang. Milly heard Inocencio open the front door and chat for a moment with Sánchez' wife and daughter. Then the voices and footsteps of the two women came toward her along the shaded, columned walk of the orchid arbor. Rodolfo Sánchez quickly found two more chairs. Graciela appeared with extra cups and saucers and a plate of pan dulce.

"Oh, Doña Milly," cried Adriana as she sank into the chair her husband provided, "not only are you spoiling us, your dulces are ruining my figure."

"Nonsense, my love!" her husband said gallantly. "You're as shapely today as you were at sixteen."

Milly turned to the daughter. "Did you go sight-seeing this morning, Yolanda, or shopping?"

"A little of both," she replied. "On the way home from the museum we went into a shop where I found a lovely silver cross with three smaller crosses hanging from it. It was attached to a strand of coral beads and was very, very old and quite wonderful."

"Did you get it?" asked her father.

"No," she said, her voice rising to a childish whine, "Mamá wouldn't buy it for me."

Milly made an effort to hide her surprise. How could a thirty-year-old woman manage to sound like a petulant twelve-year-old? There'd been no hint of sulkiness at the breakfast table this morning. Perhaps this was a special act put on for her father.

"The cross was wildly expensive, Yolanda," her mother said reasonably. "Let me do some bargaining with the shop owner. You know we left because I didn't want to appear too eager."

"But someone else may buy it in the meantime!"

"What was the name of the shop?" asked Milly.

"Casa Victor."

"Then you probably found an antique cross from the region of Yalálag. The very old ones are quite rare and the design is pre-Hispanic, so it is not a Christian cross. If you do go back for more bargaining, take my word for it that anything you find at Casa Victor is top quality and reliably authentic."

"Adriana, my love," Rodolfo Sánchez said to his wife, "I think you should get the cross for Yolanda and find something beautiful for yourself as well."

Adriana laughed coquetishly. "I wish you'd come with us, Rodolfo. You have such impeccable taste and you're so wonderfully generous. I love to go shopping with you."

I'll just bet you do, thought Milly.

"It is tempting," said Sánchez, "but I promised the doctor I would spend my entire vacation within the walls of Casa Colonial, and here I'll stay."

"You're right, of course, my love. It is very tranquil here, and God knows you need the rest."

Milly pretended to be interested in her coffee while she stored little nuggets of information in her memory. Rodolfo

Sánchez was a liar who was not well enough to leave the house. The daughter was very immature for her age. Sánchez and his wife seemed to enjoy spoiling her and each other. Apparently, money was no problem at all.

If this sort of data turned out to be unimportant, thought Milly, she could just forget about it. But if she continued soaking up whatever bits of information came her way, sooner or later she might hear something useful; something to help her deal with the problem of Rodolfo Sánchez' large, erstwhile partner.

"What business did you retire from, señor?" she asked Sánchez.

"I was an entrepreneur, señora."

"In any particular field, señor?"

"In many different areas, señora. Business is where you find it."

How neatly Sánchez had side-stepped her question. Did he have something to hide, as she suspected, or was this his polite way of telling her that she was too damned nosy? She dropped the subject, unable to think of a ladylike way to pry further into his affairs.

The doorbell rang again. As usual around this hour, guests were returning to The Casa from their morning sight-seeing.

"Con permiso," she said, and hurried down the orchid arbor toward the front door. Her feet knew every bump of the walkway and she moved with swift confidence. The bell rang a second time before she got there, so she assumed that Elpidio was at the market and Inocencio had gone to the bank. She opened the door and blinked against the brilliant sunshine.

The entire doorway seemed to be filled with someone tall and immensely wide. El Diablo? Milly gasped. She clutched the door with both hands, ready to slam it as hard as she could, when a woman's voice said amiably, "Sank you, Milly. I'm sorry ve disturb-ed you."

Just in time, Milly's shaking hands caught the door and

drew it wide to admit Olga and Poul, the placid Danish couple who were staying in number three. The husband was thin and very tall, the wife shorter, but amply upholstered. Their double silhouette had given the impression of one gigantic person.

Milly was swept with a relief so heady that it made her almost euphoric. "You're not disturbing me a bit, Olga. Come on in and tell me about your morning." She closed the door and followed them through the entryway, thinking how pleasant it would now be to sit on the veranda and have an ordinary conversation with everyday, friendly people. Poul poured his long body into one of the leather chairs and groaned with obvious contentment. Olga spun around and took a step toward Milly.

"Look!" she commanded, her voice quivering with shy excitement.

Look? Oh, dear. Milly hated to tell people that she could barely see. Their shocked sympathy was hard to take. Years ago, an ophthamologist had told her that her retinas looked like a pair of brown lace doilies. Since then, she had discovered that if she turned her head slightly, part of some object might pop into her vision; through a hole in the lace, as it were. Praying now for a momentary flash of clear sight, she turned her head to the side and back again, slowly, trying her best to focus on Olga.

The woman moved closer, an enveloping presence radiating body heat. Milly's instinct was to step away, but she quietly held her ground, hoping for some kind of visual revelation.

At last, out of the sides of her eyes Milly glimpsed a magnificent bosom at eye level and only inches away.

"Isn't it vunderful?" asked Olga.

"Stupendous," murmured Milly. She fought to control a rising giggle as she continued to gaze at the only thing she could spot; Olga's majestic bosom.

Poul said with bright enthusiasm, "It's vun of se most beautiful sings I haf ever seen!"

"I'll just bet it is!" said Milly.

"Ve found it only fifteen minutes ago at a shop downtown," said Olga.

"Amazing!" Milly compressed her lips over a bubble of laughter. "What is it?"

"It's an antique Yalálag Cross."

"Ahh!" Milly sobered at once. "Is it attached to a string of coral beads?"

"Ja, sey're coral. Isn'd it lovely?"

"I'll bet you got it at Casa Victor. Am I right?"

"Ja, Milly. How did you know?"

"Oh...just a lucky guess. You were very wise to have bought this cross, Olga. It's a beautiful thing that will grow more valuable with every passing year."

Olga and Poul went happily off to their room.

As Milly turned in the other direction and headed toward her cottage, the doorbell rang again. She threw the door wide this time.

"Hi, Milly," said a feminine voice.

Milly recognized the couple who were staying in Number Five; Billie Jo and Elmer Beamis from Tulsa, Oklahoma.

Another person seemed to be right behind them, someone who carried a large bundle. "Con permiso," said Elpidio's soft voice. He sidled past and headed for the kitchen at a run.

"Wow!" Elmer said with a laugh. "That sumbitch was in one helluva hurry."

"That was the gardener," Milly explained. "The cook must have sent him to market for something she needed right away."

"Why doesn't he use the back door?"

"Strangely enough, we don't have one. I wish we did. All the household supplies have to come through the front and across the patio. Some days it's a constant parade."

"Ne'mind," said Billie Jo, "it's interestin' to see workmen carryin' plucked chickens and bottles of water over to the kitchen. Adds local color."

"Kin I buy you a beer, Milly?" Elmer asked.

"No, thank you, Elmer."

"See you at dinner, then," he called as he and Billie Jo turned down the veranda and headed for their room.

Once again, Milly moved toward her cottage, looking forward to a spate of quiet seclusion before dinner. How clever Herbert had been to place their little hideaway at the far end of the garden. It sat close to the patio wall, nestled under a splendid cascade of bugambilla vines. The cottage was the one place where Milly felt safe from public scrutiny. Long ago she had accepted the fact that as the owner of Casa Colonial she'd be on perpetual display for the guests. She played her role by dressing with quiet flair and behaving with warmth and dignity at all times. She'd had plenty of practice and felt that she did her job well.

Inside the cottage, however, she could relax. With a grateful sigh she kicked off her shoes, ruffled her hair with her fingers and stretched mightily. She reached out to touch her talking clock. "It-is-one-oh-four-peeyem," intoned the metallic voice. She lay down on the bed, pulled her afghan up over her shoulders and reached to turn on the talking book machine. There was time for nearly an hour of reading before the two o'clock dinner bell.

The book droned along, the reader's voice occasionally drowned out by the persistent barking of a dog somewhere in the distance. It must be the dog she'd heard last night. Milly put it out of her mind and thought instead about strange old Sánchez lurking in the laundry room and then lying about it. And what about his big, disgusting ex-partner bullying Inocencio?

And then she remembered what had been the most intriguing part of the whole morning—when Amelia had displayed her weavings while Paco looked out the living room window and spied the big man's feet hanging out of the hammock. No two ways about it, Paco had been terrified by the sight of those feet. What was it he'd said? "Yesterday I met someone wearing shoes exactly like those."

What a fascinating development.

How many men in the Valley of Oaxaca would be wearing huge white shoes with purple shoelaces? Not more than one, surely. So Paco was probably acquainted with the gigantic former partner of Rodolfo Sánchez, and was afraid of him. Wise man! Next time she saw Paco she must remember to ask him about it.

The barking of the dog grew louder and more agitated. The sound swelled, as if the big animal were charging toward her across the flat roof of the house next door. The dog seemed to stop when it reached the common wall between the two properties. Milly imagined a great shaggy slavering beast standing up there, looking down into the empty lot behind her house, barking furiously and flooding her cottage with the sound of his angry voice.

This mindless violation of her sanctum caused Milly to sit up in the middle of her bed, furious, the afghan clutched around her shoulders. Over the years she had learned to accept the insistent clamor of the city of Oaxaca outside her walls, but this dog was really the limit! The animal, as if sensing her outrage, moved away, the stacatto barking gradually fading to silence.

Milly lay back on the pillow. She hoped the dog was merely a visitor next door and had not taken up permanent residence. In an effort to put it out of her mind she thought about Paco and Amelia again. Perhaps she could organize a trip to Santo Tomás Jalieza for Adriana Sánchez and her daughter, and anyone else who wanted to go along. Friday would be a good day. They could visit the Friday market at Ocotlán, then stop by Santo Tomás on the way home. She'd ask Inocencio to hire a small bus and driver, and perhaps a guide so that people wouldn't get lost in the big Ocotlán market.

Milly smiled in anticipation as she groped for her talking book machine and turned up the volume.

CHAPTER 5

Paco and Amelia climbed off the bus onto the shoulder of the road. With a blast of compressed air the folding door slammed shut behind them, almost on their heels. Paco grabbed Amelia's hand and they leapt aside as the motor roared and the ancient, dusty vehicle lumbered back onto the pavement. What was the matter with the driver? Paco wondered. Why was he in such a hurry? They watched, bewildered by this frantic departure, as the bus careened down the two-lane highway toward Ocotlán, farting thunder and clouds of black smoke. The bleat of a nannygoat tied to the roof-rack faded as the bus climbed a short hill, dropped down the other side, and disappeared into the distance.

Amelia squinted and pressed the corner of her rebozo over her mouth and nose to block the fumes.

Paco shouldered the sack of Amelia's weaving and said urgently, "*Vámonos a la casa!*" Let's go home.

They crossed the highway and hurried down the narrow dirt road that wound between fields of spindly castor bean plants. When they reached the edge of the town plaza, they found it deserted. Paco had expected a crowd of federales to still be there. He came to a nervous halt and felt Amelia edge closer to him.

"Listen!" he whispered.

"I don't hear anything," Amelia whispered back.

"Neither do I. That's what worries me."

Birds chirped in the Indian laurel tree whose generous branches sheltered the market area of the plaza. Far away a rooster crowed. But not one human voice could be heard. Not even a radio.

"Where is everyone?" whispered Amelia.

"I don't know."

"Why am I so frightened?"

Paco didn't answer. Instead of crossing the grassy plaza diagonally, as they usually did, he led the way around its perimeter, walking rapidly and staying close to the walls of adobe houses that fronted the dusty street. For some reason that he did not stop to analyze, today he would have felt exposed out in the center of the open plaza.

As they passed the gate to the churchyard, two federales appeared suddenly from behind the adobe wall.

"*Alto!*" one of them shouted. Halt!

Paco shied like a startled horse, his heart pounding. Behind him Amelia gasped.

The two soldiers were very young, teenagers probably. They blocked the way, standing spraddle-legged in the street in their polished boots and ill-fitting green cotton uniforms. They clutched their rifles in front of them with both hands, caressing the triggers uncertainly. Paco sensed anxiety and a potential for violence in these two, and he eyed the firearms with great trepidation.

"Where do you think you're going?" challenged the older of the two boys. His voice cracked a little on the last word.

Paco fought down a wild flash of hysterical laughter. It was unnerving to be challenged by children.

"We're going to our casa, señor," he answered politely. "We live in this pueblo." He hesitated, longing to find out what had happened. Curiosity overcame prudence. "Do you mind if I ask a question?"

44

"Ask."

"Why are you here, señor? Has there been some trouble while we were away?"

"That's none of your business."

Of course it's my business, thought Paco. This is my town. But he said nothing.

"What have you got there?" demanded the soldier, pointing at Amelia's sack with his chin.

"It's only my wife's weaving."

"Take a look, *joven*," the fellow said to his companion. "I'll cover you."

Paco handed over the sack. He knew it contained perfectly ordinary things, so why did he suddenly feel panicky and short of breath? It had something to do with his cornfield, perhaps. Night before last. He forced these thoughts from his mind.

The younger man rummaged inside the sack and handed it back to Paco. "I'll keep these," he said. He handed one of Amelia's handwoven belts to his friend and stuffed the other into his own pocket. He gazed at Paco steadily, as if daring him to object.

"Move along," said the other soldier, gesturing with his rifle.

"Come on," Paco whispered to Amelia, and they hurried down the street toward home. Paco, filled with foreboding, strode ahead. Amelia had to break into a trot now and then to keep up. Teresa, their neighbor and Amelia's best friend, peeked out her door at them, but turned away without speaking.

From the patio gate, Paco could see his father sitting very straight on his wooden chair under the copal tree.

"Paco, thank God you're home," the old man cried, and struggled to his feet.

"Are you all right, Father?"

"Where are the children?" Amelia asked breathlessly.

"The children are at school, Amelia. We're all fine, but I'm glad you're home. After you left this morning, the federales came through town and searched every house. It was terrible."

"We saw a crowd of them at the bus stop when we left for Oaxaca, and now there are two youngsters standing guard in the plaza. Do you know why they're here, Father?"

"Yes, I do!" Paco's father glanced about uneasily and dropped his voice almost to a whisper. "I have a terrible fear that I was responsible for the whole thing."

"Shhh," said Paco, "let's go into the house where we can talk." He led the way through the door and over to the far side of the room.

"Now tell me what whole thing you're responsible for, Father."

"Do you remember, Paco, two days ago I said that in the dark of night we should carry the corpse of the rich man down to the bus stop and sit him on the bench?"

"My memory has been erased, Father, but I'm listening." Paco felt his gut tighten. He frowned and shook his head a little to warn his father to speak even more softly.

"I was only joking when I said that, my son, I swear it! But they tell me that this morning the corpse was there. Sitting on the bench. Dead. Even though you buried him. A bus driver called the police. Now the whole village is under suspicion and it's my fault."

No wonder the bus had dumped them out on the roadside and sped away so fast just now, thought Paco. The driver had been afraid to stop at this unlucky place.

Paco asked gently, "Did you put the body on the bench, Father?"

"Of course not, my son. You know I didn't!"

"Then how could it be your fault?"

"Oh, Paco, I don't know. Did I say the joke too loudly? Perhaps some bad person overheard and accepted the idea. Or perhaps some *nahual*, some wicked spirit, came in the night to play a joke on all of us. It's confusing. Frightening."

Amelia murmured softly, "Tell me, dear Father, are you

sure it was the rich man from out of the cornfield? Did you actually see the corpse?"

"No, my daughter, I was not permitted to look at the body they found on the bench. But who else could it be?" He threw his hands into the air and shook his head.

Paco struck his forehead with the heel of his hand. "I know who it was," he groaned. "You see, Father, there were actually two dead bodies. We won't talk about the first one because it is all taken care of. The second one appeared in the cornfield yesterday. I didn't mention it because I was trying to put it out of my mind."

"Who was it?" asked Grandfather.

"It was a farmer, younger than me, and someone I didn't know. He and the rich man were both murdered by a cruel giant."

"Holy Mother of God!" whispered Amelia, crossing herself. "Did you see him do it?"

"No, I didn't. But there's no question in my mind that he killed them."

Paco's father leaned forward to peer into his son's face. "A giant?" he asked incredulously. "Do you mean a real giant?"

Paco nodded. "I don't know his name, but he's real. He was waiting for me when I arrived at the corn field yesterday morning. I told him he'd have to dispose of the second body himself," Paco confessed ruefully, "and he must have put it on the bench at the bus stop."

"What does this fellow want from you, Paco?" asked his father.

"He told me he's my partner now, and he says I must plant marijuana instead of corn."

"Are you going to do it?" asked Amelia.

"Absolutely not!" replied Paco. "Well, not unless I have to," he ammended miserably. "I'm afraid this giant will kill me if I don't do what he says."

"Madre de dios!"

"He swears that he and I can both get rich by growing marijuana."

"Don't believe him," Amelia said flatly. "It's a lie."

"I know it is, Amelia. Anyway, marijuana is illegal and I don't want to go to jail. But I don't want him to shoot me, either!"

"Stand firm, mi hijo," Paco's father said, placing a resolute hand on his son's shoulder. "Remember that the devil often appears as a *mestizo* who tempts men with the promise of money. Now tell me, Paco, how will I know this fellow if I see him?"

"Oh, you'll know him, Father! He must be the tallest man in the world, taller even than a doorway. He's very, very wide and he has a black beard. Each of his feet is as big as the *metate* Amelia uses for grinding the corn, and he wears white shoes with purple shoelaces."

"Oh!" said Amelia. "The man in the hammock at Casa Colonial! That's why you were so nervous when we were there. Paco, we must warn Doña Milly."

"Yes," said Paco, feeling guilty, "I should have warned her this morning, but I was too frightened."

Unaccountably, his father began to laugh. Paco glared at the old man. What could possibly be so funny?

"My son, I have just realized how ridiculous this situation is."

Paco said stiffly, "It is not just ridiculous, Father, it is dangerous."

"Of course it's dangerous, mi hijo, and it can lead to bad trouble for the whole family. But there is humor here. Think about it, Paco. You have been commanded to break the law in partnership with the most conspicuous rascal in the state of Oaxaca; a man who can't even walk around without calling attention to himself! I ask you, my son, how can such a person raise marijuana, or do anything else, in secret?"

Clearly, Grandfather was trying to lift their spirits as he always did. Paco tried his best to smile, but could only grimace as he imagined the giant tip-toeing through the marijuana fields on his metate feet, towering over the plants like a papier mache gigante in a church procession. The image was so frightening because in Santo Tomás Jalieza, as in all Zapotec villages in the Valley of Oaxaca, everyone was short. There was scarcely anyone over five and a half feet tall, and no one had a beard. El Gigante, on the other hand, was so big that he'd have to duck his head and turn his massive shoulders sideways to get into a house.

Paco forced a grin. "You're right, Father," he said. "That man sticks out like—*Dios mío!*—like a marijuana bush in a cornfield!" He and his father threw their arms around each other and rocked with silent laughter. How good it felt to laugh, if only for a moment.

"Mi hijo," said Paco's father, pulling away and pretending to admonish him, "if you must become a criminal, for God's sweet sake go into business with some sneaky little weasel, not a man who's built like a steam locomotive!"

Amelia giggled nervously.

"Let's forget about him," Paco said, still feigning cheerfulness. "If we're lucky, the federales will scare him away and we'll never see him again."

The grandfather cocked his head to one side with a quizzical smile.

Amelia said skeptically, "That will be only if we're *very* lucky."

Paco found that he could no longer look the two of them in the eyes, for he felt certain that El Gigante would soon reappear. He turned his back and walked outside, lifting his eyes to the eastern hills from force of habit. The clouds had gathered and a heavy storm was coming. A gust of cold wind rattled the trees. Paco shivered.

49

CHAPTER 6

Late in the afternoon, Milly came out of her cottage and headed for the office. As she sank into the chair by Inocencio's desk he barked at her, "I want you to talk to your guests about the water right away."

Milly's hackles rose at the peremptory tone. Why did Inocencio sometimes act as if *she* worked for *him*? She opened her mouth to put him in his place, then thought better of it as she realized that he sounded more distraught than arrogant.

She spoke calmly. "I've already told them not to drink the water, Inocencio. What's the matter, did someone get sick?"

"I'm not talking about *drinking* the water. I mean that someone left a faucet running today, and the big *tinaco* emptied, so there was no water for the kitchen all afternoon."

"Oh, dear! Yes, I'll warn everyone to turn faucets off tight, and I'll tell the muchachas to check the bathrooms every morning after people leave for the day."

"That won't work, they'll forget. I guess I'll have to check all the guest bathrooms myself."

Poor Inocencio. He had enough to do without adding this to his list of duties. But water was an ongoing problem.

It seemed that no one in Oaxaca had ever heard of a pressure system. Almost every roof in town held a tinaco, a water storage tank. At Casa Colonial, city water dribbled into a group of connected, roof-top tinacos at very low pressure. From there it descended by gravity into the laundry, kitchen, and bathrooms. If there was a steady leak anywhere in the line, the tinacos gradually emptied and took hours to refill.

Inocencio snapped at her again. "Unfortunately, señora, your pipes are old and incompetent."

Milly, startled by this seemingly personal turn of the conversation, tried to keep from laughing. She pressed her lips together firmly, looked away and and strove for dignity.

"You're right, Inocencio. My old pipes are quite a problem."

The telephone rang and Inocencio jumped out of his chair to answer it. It was a wrong number, but by the time he returned, he was more calm. "Elpidio always thinks he keeps everything in perfect working order, but he's not a very good plumber."

"I know," she murmured sympathetically. "Margarita is better at making repairs than he is. I often ask her to fix the toilets when she comes on duty at night, but even Margarita can't work miracles."

"Things keep breaking down because new parts are such poor quality nowadays."

"Well, when I go up to Iowa in May, I'll bring back a suitcase full of ballcock assemblies and faucet washers. Doggone it," she laughed, "every year it's something different. Remember last May when I brought home the lawn sprinkler? The customs people in Mexico City thought it was a bomb and questioned me so persistently that I almost missed the airplane to Oaxaca."

Inocencio said, "Speaking of airplanes, I forgot to tell you that there are some new guests coming in tonight."

"Will they get here in time for supper?"

"No. They'll take the eight o'clock flight out of Mexico

City, so you won't see them here until nine-thirty or ten. I'm going home early, but Margarita knows what to do. There will be two adults and a ten-year-old child and they've asked for one room, only."

"Better put them in the *cochera*," suggested Milly.

The cochera was the large guest room between the front door and the old "coach" entrance that opened onto the street. The room was close to the office, but isolated from the rest of the house, and held a king-size bed and one single. It was ideal for a couple traveling with a child.

"I'll try to stay up till they come," she added, "but I make no guarantees. I'm usually in bed and asleep by nine."

Graciela served stuffed *chayotes* for supper. The buttered-crumb topping was crisp, the filling so rich and savory that Milly asked for seconds. She could have sworn she heard Herbert whisper, *Thunder-thighs!* but maybe it was her own conscience. God, if that didn't take all the fun out of eating, nothing would. I'll skip dessert, she vowed to herself. Then Ramona put mango ice cream and crisp, honeyed *buñuelos* in front of her, and it was all over.

Milly did her best to stay up, but by the time the new guests arrived, she was already in bed and fast asleep. She roused when she heard the big front door slam, then dozed off again.

Much later, the dog next door began to bark. The sound brought Milly bolt upright in bed, as if she were a puppet and someone had jerked her strings. The tumultuous racket almost prevented her from hearing the time. It-is-one-fifty-two-ayem, said the impassive voice of her talking clock.

Milly threw herself back on the pillow, certain that the stupid dog was disturbing all her guests. This sort of thing was very bad for business. But in a minute or two, the barking stopped. Perhaps the dog's owner had ordered him to be quiet. No use worrying, she decided. She turned her pillow, punched it to a comfortable fit, and went back to sleep.

An hour later, the dog barked again. By now, Milly was

furious. If the bedlam continued every hour, all night, she'd be a wreck by morning. This time, after the barking stopped, she had some difficulty getting back to sleep.

When next she opened her eyes, sunshine streamed through the windows of her cottage. She showered and dressed, resolved to do something drastic about the dog.

She found Elpidio in the garden, watering the poinsettias.

"Buenos días, Elpidio. How are you this morning?"

"Buenos días, patrona. I'm another day older, but otherwise fine."

Milly smiled. This was the silly game she and Elpidio played almost every morning. It was his considerate way of letting her know that she was not the only one growing older, that he too, was feeling the passage of time. Since he was young enough to be her grandson, she found his effort touching and rather amusing.

"Elpidio, I have a problem. Will you help me?"

"Certainly, patrona."

"There is a new dog next door," she said, pointing in that direction, "and he makes a tremendous noise when he barks. It sounds as if he's up on the roof. Is that possible?"

"Sí, patrona, it is possible. Many people keep a watchdog on the roof."

"Por favor, can you find out if the dog is a visitor? If he is only visiting our neighbor, I won't complain."

"Sí, patrona. I know the man who lives there. I'll ask him and let you know."

Milly went on to the dining room. Just inside the door, she found people sitting at one of the small tables. Almost no one ever sat there. These must be the newcomers.

"I'm Doña Milly," she said with her friendliest smile, "the owner of Casa Colonial. Come and join me at the big table. I'm afraid you'll be lonesome if you stay over here all by yourselves."

She sat at her usual place with her back to the kitchen door. The room was sunny and warm and smelled comfortably of coffee, bacon, and chile peppers. Graciela had set the table with the new yellow place mats from Santo Tomás and the blue and white plates from Guadalajara. There was a centerpiece of red flowers, probably poinsettias.

The newcomers found chairs on her left. So far they were the only people in the room, besides herself, and so far they hadn't said a word.

"There's fresh fruit and coffee on the sideboard," Milly said. "Oatmeal, too, with raisins in it. Please help yourselves. Then one of the muchachas will take your orders for eggs."

"Oh, boy, oatmeal," said the man. "I haven't had oatmeal for years." He pushed back his chair and walked over to the sideboard.

"Oh, *yuck*," said the child. "I want Pop-Tarts."

The woman said, "I don't think they have Pop-Tarts here, Leslie."

"As far as I know, there aren't any Pop-Tarts in the entire state of Oaxaca," said Milly, "but we do have fresh *bolillos* and strawberry jam and wonderful hot chocolate."

Was she talking to a boy or a girl? In her family, Leslie was a favorite girl's name, but this child sounded more like a boy. Nowadays, she supposed, people would say the name was unisex. What a revolting word.

"Where do you live, Leslie?" she asked.

"I live with my mother, but I *wish* it was with my father."

Obviously this rather unpleasant child had learned to play off one divorced parent against the other. "I meant what *town* do you live in, dear," Milly said gently.

"Redwood City," replied the child. "I bet you don't even know where that is."

"Sure I do. Redwood City is in California, south of San Francisco, and right down the road from Palo Alto and Stanford University. Palo Alto is Oaxaca's sister city. I'll bet you didn't know that."

"Of course I do," said Leslie with lofty disdain. "There's a boy from Oaxaca in our school this year, and he told me all about it."

"Are you on vacation from school?"

"No, we're running away."

The woman cut in swiftly, sounding embarrassed. "I took him out of school for a couple of weeks. I thought he'd probably learn more by coming to Oaxaca than he would by staying in the classroom."

"I do believe you're right," murmured Milly. At least she now knew that Leslie was a boy. Later she'd make it a point to find out what Leslie and his mother were running away from. She smiled at the mother. "And what is your name?" she asked.

"Oh, sorry! My name is Evelyn."

"And I'm George," said the man as he returned to the table.

The dining room began to fill with the other guests. As they brought coffee and plates of fresh fruit from the sideboard, they said good morning to Milly and she introduced George, Evelyn, and Leslie. Sánchez' daughter, Yolanda, was the last to arrive. She seemed grumpy. Not a morning person, obviously.

When the muchachas had finished serving, Milly said, "I've ordered a bus and an English-speaking guide for nine o'clock Friday morning, and you're all invited to take a trip with me out into the valley."

"Dot's vunderful, Milly," said Poul's deep voice. "Vhere are ve going?"

"First we'll go to the outdoor market at Ocotlán. Then we'll visit a very famous potter who makes interesting figures of women. Personally, I think they're all self portraits! And then we'll go to Santo Tomás Jalieza to buy place mats."

"Like these?" asked Billie Jo. "I wondered where these mats came from. Are they expensive?"

"Who cares?" muttered Leslie. "They're ugly."

"Hush!" ordered Evelyn.

Milly spoke across Leslie to Billie Jo. "No, they're only a couple of dollars each," she said. "The women weave them on backstrap looms just as they have for over two thousand years."

"Two thousand years of ug-*ly*," whispered Leslie.

Milly ignored him.

"Are place mats traditional?" inquired Adriana. "Surely the Zapotecs don't use placemats in their homes."

"Not as far as I know," replied Milly. "Traditionally—in olden times—only belts were woven in Santo Tomás. Belts used to be very important because the traditional skirt is just a long piece of fabric wound around a woman's body and held in place by a belt tied very tightly. Nowadays traditional costumes are mostly worn on special occasions, so there's not much of a market for belts anymore."

"Why do they make place mats if they don't use them?" asked Leslie.

"They sell them for money to buy food and clothing," Milly replied. "A few years ago I asked the women to make some place mats for me. They had to adapt their looms to the correct width, and it was quite a job, but now they crank out place mats by the hundreds for tourists."

"What do the men of the village do?" asked Yolanda.

"They raise corn and other foods for their familes and help sell the weaving. By the way," she asked, "did anyone hear the dog barking in the middle of the night?"

There was a general murmur of denial around the table.

Milly was relieved to learn that she was the only one who'd been bothered by the noise. She'd rest easier tonight knowing that no one else would be disturbed if the dog set up another ruckus.

As she crossed the patio after breakfast, Elpidio called to her. "Excuse me, patrona. A moment ago I talked to my friend next door about the barking dog. My friend says the dog is not a visitor. It belongs to him and has lived right there on his roof for four years."

"Four years! And I never heard it before? How strange."

"Sí, patrona, it is very strange—or perhaps it is very lucky!" He laughed. "My friend is a very comical person.

He always tells me jokes."

"What joke did he tell you today, Elpidio?"

"He told me that he calls his dog Apollo Thirteen."

"Apollo Thirteen? Why does he call him that?"

"Because every time the dog sees a cat he goes straight up in the air like a rocket ship. WHOOSH—Apollo Thirteen!" Elpidio doubled over with laughter.

Milly didn't think it was all that funny, but Elpidio's merriment was contagious and she joined in, giggling with delight. "Maybe Apollo Thirteen saw a cat in our vacant lot last night," she said. "I hope he doesn't spot one tonight because I need my sleep."

CHAPTER 7

For three days Paco had been harvesting his phenom- enal corn crop. Over and over he had cut enough dry stalks with his machete to make up a load, then bound them together with rope twisted from maguey fibers. He'd bent forward, dragged the heavy butt ends of the corn up over his shoulders, passed the rope over a pad on his fore- head, and staggered toward home, the tips of the long stalks trailing on the ground behind him. He was resigned to the pain and sweat because that was his lot in life, and because hard work put food in his children's bellies.

Now, as Paco struggled to drag a particularly heavy load through the patio gate, Amelia ran to help him. He stepped back, slid free of the rope and tipped his load onto the ground. Together he and Amelia strained to shift the huge bundle, dragging it over to the back wall of the patio and releasing it beside the towering pile of cornstalks already there. Working again side by side with Amelia made him think of that terrible night in the cornfield. He forced the thought from his mind. That particular memory had been erased by Don Porfirio, he reminded himself.

"How many more loads?" asked Amelia.

"This is the last, gracias a dios!"

"There is cool water in the basin," she said. "Wash yourself, Paco, and rest a bit. Whenever you're ready, we'll have supper."

The basin stood on a box beside the door of the house. Paco took off his dirty shirt and used a gourd to sluice water over his head and shoulders repeatedly. He pretended that he was leaning into a small waterfall down at the river. The water felt blissfully cool against his skin. He shook his head, finger-combed his wet hair and struggled into a clean shirt.

Refreshed and at peace, Paco turned toward his family and found himself staring into the coldly smiling face of El Gigante. While Paco had been splashing under an imaginary waterfall, the man had sneaked through the gate and had taken over Grandfather's chair. Sitting down he was low enough to be face to face with Paco.

A surge of despair made Paco's shoulders slump and his body feel leaden. He was not really surprised to see El Gigante, for all along he'd known in his heart that the man would return, but at this particular moment Paco felt too weary to cope with the enemy seated before him.

"Hola, Paquito, my little partner," said El Gigante in a jolly rumble. "I see that you have completed a wonderful harvest."

Paco groaned inwardly. He did not reply.

"I have come to help you celebrate. I'm staying for supper."

Paco glanced at Amelia. She peered into the kettle simmering on the fire, gave it a stir, then shrugged.

"We have only *caldo de pollo negro* in the pot, señor." Paco wondered if a man from the city could grasp the meaning of this statement. Caldo de pollo negro—literally, black chicken soup—was the local way of pointing out that chicken might be the poor man's meat, but black beans were the truly poor man's chicken. "It is simple food," he added, "but we will share what we have."

Amelia spoke softly to Julia, who then handed their

guest a large crisp tortilla and a bowl of beans. Immediately, he began to eat. Grandfather was served next, then Paco and the boys. By that time, El Gigante had cleaned his bowl and handed it back to Julia for seconds. Paco cringed at such bad manners. He noticed that Amelia was already scraping the bottom of the pot and that she and Julia were not eating at all. With a pig at the trough, there was not enough to go around.

"When will you plow and plant again, Paquito?" asked the giant, sauce dribbling down his chin and into his beard.

"I'm not sure, señor," hedged Paco, although he knew very well. "It depends on the shape and position of the moon. Don Porfirio, the brujo, will advise me."

The big man chuckled. "I think it will be soon," he said, "and so I have brought the seeds you agreed to plant."

"I did not agree to anything, señor," Paco reminded him.

El Gigante popped the last of his tortilla into his mouth. While he chewed, he ran his enormous finger over the bottom of the bowl and around the sides. He put the finger into his mouth and sucked it noisily while he held the empty bowl out to Julia.

The child approached with courtesy, as she had been taught. When she reached out to take the bowl, he drew it back just far enough to force her one step closer, and then another. When she finally grasped the bowl, he refused to let it go. Puzzled, she looked to her mother for guidance.

Quickly the man scooped Julia onto his lap and looked over her head at Paco. He jerked his finger from his mouth with a sound like a cow pulling its foot out of the mud.

Paco felt such outrage that he thought his eyes might bulge out of his head. No man ever touched another's wife or daughters. Such disrespect was unspeakable. It was grounds for violence! For murder! He looked to Grandfather and the boys for help, but they were staring in horror at little Julia trapped on the giant's lap. Sick with fear and frustration, Paco was forced to acknowledge bitterly that the family was powerless. Even if they were all to attack at once, it would be futile.

"Here are the seeds," said El Gigante, and he tossed a small cotton sack onto the ground at Paco's feet. Then he slid his hand up Julia's leg and under her skirt.

Julia whimpered and gazed imploringly at her father.

El Gigante smiled his terrible cold smile and winked at Paco. "Pick up the seeds, Paquito," he urged gently.

Paco stooped, picked up the bag of seeds and tucked it under his arm. He strode toward the giant. "I'll be planting on Thursday," he said, his voice hoarse. He reached out for Julia who lifted her arms to him. Paco set her on the ground and she ran to her mother.

"Muy bien, Paquito. I'll check back with you on Thursday." El Gigante smiled at Julia and licked his full lips.

The child threw her arms around her mother's waist. Amelia held her close and they turned away.

"Thanks for supper," said the giant. "*Hasta luego*." He strolled out the patio gate and down the street toward the plaza.

No one moved until he was out of sight. Then Grandfather hobbled over to his chair and collapsed onto it. "I've lived so long that I thought I'd seen everthing," he wailed, "but I never imagined *this*. The world is getting to be a terrible place! What are we going to do?"

For a moment, Paco was unable to speak. His whole body shook with anger and humiliation. He threw down the sack of marijuana seeds, then turned his back on the family and closed his eyes for several moments. Gradually, he grew more calm. At last he opened his eyes and looked over his shoulder at Amelia.

"The first thing we're going to do is arrange an escape route," he said. "I'll get some melon crates and we'll stack them by the back wall. Any time that man comes here, Amelia, I want you and the children—the boys too—to climb over the wall and *run*. Go to Don Porfirio's house. I'll make arrangements for him to hide you."

Amelia nodded crisply. "Are you going to plant the marijuana?"

"I'll have to," said Paco, looking at his daughter. "There isn't any choice."

He turned to the east, raising his eyes toward the mountains. All his life he had drawn courage and comfort from the eternal hills. Now, when he needed their strength so desperately, they appeared sullen and seemed to have drawn away into the evening mists. Paco sraightened his shoulders and faced his family again.

Amelia was scrubbing the bean pot with even more than her usual vigor. She paused, sat back on her heels and squinted at Paco. "I am terribly frightened," she said with a shudder, "but I believe that God will give our family the strength to do whatever we have to do."

Paco nodded, wishing he shared Amelia's certainty.

"But there is something else worrying me," Amelia went on, "a problem outside our family. I'm thinking of Doña Milly. Four days ago that wicked man was in her hammock!"

"You're right," agreed Paco, "we must find a way to warn her about him."

"Tomorrow is market day," Amelia continued. "If Doña Milly brings her tourists here, I can tell her about him then."

"But if she does not come tomorrow," said Paco, "then we must go back to Casa Colonial. It is our responsibility to let her know that El Gigante is a dangerous man. She must never let him into her house again."

CHAPTER 8

Milly sat on the front seat, right behind the driver. As he tooled the small bus expertly along the highway toward Santo Tomás, he whistled an expanded, flowery version of "Cielito Lindo." Milly chimed in, amusing herself by whistling her part in harmony. It had been Herbert's favorite Mexican song, she recalled with nostalgia. At the end of the chorus, to her amazement, the driver segued into "The Last Time I Saw Paris." Milly discovered that she couldn't whistle with a smile on her face, and gave it up. Where had he learned this song? she wondered. Television?

All the Casa Colonial guests except Rodolfo Sánchez and the bosomy Olga had accepted Milly's invitation for this special Friday outing. For Sánchez to decline was no surprise. He was sticking to his resolve to spend his entire vacation within the walls of Casa Colonial. It was too bad about Olga, though. Poul explained that Olga was worn out from sightseeing and prefered to relax at home. Milly said she understood.

The group had just come from a visit to the famous potter, Josefina Aguilár. Before that, the guide had led them through the intricate passageways of the Ocotlán market, past the pottery, the sombreros, the baskets, the blaring music of tape vendors, the ear-splitting voices of men hawking patent medicines, and finally to the animals. Barnyard sounds and odors were quite familiar to Milly. She had lived on a farm most of her married life. Here in the market, pigs grunted and squealed, roosters crowed, a burro wheezed and groaned. She had stumbled along behind young Pepe, the guide, clinging to his belt with one hand, marching in step so she wouldn't tread on his heels, and loving every moment of the adventure.

Now, as the bus left the highway and swerved onto the side road leading to Santo Tomás, she was tossed against the window momentarily. Riding in any vehicle was frustrating for Milly. She couldn't see the road ahead, so was unable to anticipate and brace herself for twists and turns. It wasn't far to the town plaza, she consoled herself.

As Pepe helped her off the bus she wondered how the Santo Tomás market could seem so peaceful. For one thing, it was very small, the whole area shaded by two huge trees. For another, no voices were raised. Nothing was sold here but weaving, and all two dozen or so weavers had much the same articles for sale. Each woman charged the same as her neighbors, so no one was bargaining. Vendors were eager, but shy. Here, buyers made choices by color, not price.

"Could you help me, please?" Billie Jo asked Milly. "I've already found some placemats I want, but I can't understand what the weaver is saying to me."

"Show me where they are," said Milly. "I'll be glad to help."

A child's voice cut in. "Never mind, ladies, I'll take care of it!" Leslie! He elbowed his way between the two women, treading on Milly's instep in the process.

Milly made a grab at the officious little twit, but missed. He and Billie Jo walked off together. If Milly wanted to find out what was going to happen next, she had no choice but to follow as best she could. Her foot hurt where Leslie had tromped on it. Angrily she limped along behind. In a moment, she heard Leslie say in perfect Spanish, "Buenas tardes, señora. This lady would like to buy your placemats, but she does not understand Spanish. Tell me, please, how much do they cost?"

"They are one hundred thirty pesos, young man, for a set of eight *mantelitos*."

"It's about twenty dollars for eight mats," reported Leslie. "Do you have a hundred and thirty pesos?"

"I have two hundred," said Billie Jo. "Does she have change?"

Leslie completed the negotiations expertly and thanked the vendor for her patience.

Milly heard Poul's voice say, "Will you help me, please, Milly?" She turned to him with a smile, happy to be needed.

"Hey, dude, I want to do it!" said Leslie, and he took Poul off in another direction.

Again Milly trailed along, more than a little miffed at having her role usurped by this precocious brat. In her mind she heard Herbert laughing at her.

The most difficult instrument to play with grace is second fiddle, he said.

Yeah, I know, Milly replied, shaking her head. And then as she turned away she felt Leslie's hot, sticky little hand slip into hers.

"That was fun," he said.

"You certainly did take over," Milly observed drily. "Where did you learn to speak Spanish so fluently?"

"At school. When I stay with my father in San Diego, I go to a bilingual school. I really like it. But I get to stay with him only half the time, so my Spanish isn't as good as it could be."

"I think you speak very well, Leslie. And now will you help me? I'm looking for a weaver named Amelia."

"Yeah, sure. I've noticed that you can't see worth a darn, so I guess you need me pretty bad."

Damn the child, Milly thought, and stifled an urge to whack him.

When they found Amelia, she put her arms around Milly in a gentle *abrazo*, that formal Mexican greeting halfway between a hug and a shoulder pat.

"Oh, señora," she murmured, "*Qué milagro!* What a miracle that you are here. I was hoping you'd come today, for I have something very important to tell you." She spoke to someone in Zapotec, the words soft, sibilant, then said to Milly in Spanish, "Julia and the American boy will take care of the booth while I'm gone. Please, señora, let's go for a short walk so no one can overhear us." She led Milly over to one side, behind the trunk of the biggest tree.

"Are the federales still here?" asked Milly, "Or is Santo Tomás quiet and peaceful again?"

"The federales have gone, gracias a dios, but our lives are far from peaceful. Now we have another problem."

"What is that, Amelia?"

"Señora, the big man with purple shoe laces—the one who was in your hammock the other day—has come to Santo Tomás."

Milly shuddered. "I don't like that man," she said. "I'm afraid of him."

"You are right to fear him, señora. He is a very dangerous person."

"I'm not surprised to hear it. From the moment I first met him I could tell that he was wicked, but how do you know him, Amelia, and what is he doing here in Santo Tomás?"

"It's a long story, señora. The important thing, the thing I must make sure you understand, is that he is evil. Please promise me that you will never let him into Casa Colonial again. This is very important for your safety."

"I'm sure you're right, Amelia! Thank you for warning me."

It did not escape Milly's notice that her question about El Diablo's connection to Paco and Amelia had been side-stepped. Perhaps she needed to be more direct and insistent. She knew that Amelia might avoid the question again, but she also knew that Amelia, a Zapotec, would never tell an outright lie.

"Amelia," she said, "explain to me, por favor, exactly what is going on. Is this bad man bothering you and Paco?"

"Only a little bit, señora."

"Then why does he worry you?"

"I can't talk about that, señora. Paco told me not to."

How frustrating this was. There was a big problem, that much was clear, but she was not allowed to know anything about it. Obviously Paco and Amelia were in deep trouble, but she couldn't help them because they wouldn't tell her what the difficulty was. Milly's personal approach to any quandry was to meet it head-on. This time she found herself groping for facts through the fog of secrecy that seemed to envelop El Diablo. Rather wildly, as she cast about in her mind for some crumb of information to build on, her memory dredged up El Diablo's association with Rodolfo Sánchez. At once she connected this to Sánchez' odd question about growing marijuana in the Casa gardens.

"Amelia," she blurted, "does your problem with the big man have anything to do with marijuana?"

There was a shocked silence for several heartbeats. The answer came at last in a whisper: "How did you know, señora?"

"I didn't know, Amelia. I only guessed. But I think the big man is the business partner of one of my guests at Casa Colonial, and...well...it's very complicated and very upsetting." This was much too vague, Milly decided. A little drama seemed in order. Experimentally she took a deep breath and let it out in an exaggerated, tremulous sigh.

Amelia responded by hugging her protectively. "Pobrecita," she whispered.

With only a slight twinge of conscience, Milly offered her sweetest smile and allowed her chin to wobble a little. "My dear Amelia, I would never ask you to go against your husband's wishes, but let me point out that if I know what's happening, maybe we can help each other. Would it be better if I'd ask Paco to tell me about it?"

There was another pause, even longer this time.

Finally Amelia said, "Doña Milly, if I talk to you about this, will you promise not to tell Paco?"

"Yes, Amelia. I promise."

"Then I will describe our troubles, señora, even though Paco told me not to." She spoke so softly that Milly had to lean forward to hear.

"El Gigante has ordered Paco to plant his fields with one row of marijuana for every two rows of corn."

"But Paco could go to jail if the federales catch him growing marijuana! He's not going to do it, is he?"

"He doesn't want to, señora, but he has to."

"Why, Amelia? *Why* does he have to?"

Amelia leaned closer still and murmured, "If Paco does not plant the seeds, terrible things will happen to our children."

Oh, God! Milly had never heard of such a disgusting threat, at least not in real life. She'd read of similar situations on some of her talking books, but those were fiction, and she customarily skipped the unpleasant parts. It was hard to accept that this was real. Her thoughts raced as she tried to examine the situation from every possible angle. If she were in the United States, she'd simply call the police. Here the police were probably in the pay of either Sánchez or El Diablo. Or both!

She could think of only one way to help her friends. "I hope you will send the children to my house until this is over," she said. "If you do, I promise that we'll take excellent care of them and keep them safe."

"Gracias, señora, that is very kind of you. However, for a man like El Gigante, Oaxaca is not a large town: he would find them! He has visited Casa Colonial once already, has he not? I would not want to endanger you and your guests, señora. I'll mention your offer to Paco and...we'll see."

Milly got the message. El Diablo had connections to

Casa Colonial, so why send the children there? Amelia preferred to keep her family with her, to protect them herself. Milly quite understood. If she were in Amelia's shoes, she'd feel the same way.

"Maybe he won't actually harm the children," Milly said. "Maybe he's just trying to frighten you."

"Then he has succeeded, señora. I'm very frightened and I believe he would not hesitate to destroy all of us. He has made his threat very plain, and Paco and I know that he has already killed two people."

"*Two people!* How do you know? Who were they?"

"I don't know who they were, señora. Paco told me about it and I don't think he knows their names. But he is very sure of what happened, and I believe him."

"So do I," said Milly in a small voice.

As she continued to turn this dreadful information in her mind, her emotions gradually steadied and her thinking grew more focused. She began to wonder why El Diablo was picking on Paco. Out of all the people in the valley, why had he chosen poor little Paco to grow marijuana for him? It didn't seem sensible unless Paco had far more land than she knew about.

"How many hectares does Paco farm?" she asked.

"Almost two hectares, señora," Amelia said proudly.

Milly did some fast mental arithmetic. One hectare was about two and a half acres, so Paco had less than five acres under cultivation. Part of that was probably in castor beans, the local cash crop. If two thirds of the remainder were planted to corn, that would leave a little over one acre for marijuana. El Diablo, who appeared to be a big-time Mexico City hoodlum, would want production from many hectares. He'd never be satisfied with profits from Paco's one measly acre. So where else could he obtain the quantities of marijuana he was looking for? Was it possible, she wondered excitedly, that he was recruiting other farmers besides Paco?

"Have you discussed this with your friends, Amelia?"

"No, señora, Paco told me not to speak of it."

"I think you should talk with one or two of your best friends, women you trust. Ask them if the giant has told their husbands to plant marijuana. I'll bet he has! It's even possible that the entire village is working for him, and you're all afraid to mention it to each other."

Out of the side of her eye, Milly could see Amelia's head move up and down, nodding in agreement. To be persuasive, Milly knew that in spite of her mounting excitement she'd have to speak like a Zapotec, her voice low and slow, her tone reasonable.

"If everyone is afraid to talk about the giant, then he has you all in his power. Any one family is too weak to bring him down, but the whole village working together would be stronger than he is: together you could drive him out of Santo Tomás Jalieza and get rid of him forever. Amelia, if you and Paco try to fight the giant alone, you can't possibly win. Talk to your friends!"

"I think you're right, señora."

"I don't know that I'm *right*, Amelia, but I do know that it's better to try than to give up without a struggle. And it's usually safest to work quietly—behind the trees, one might say. Just as we're doing now," she added with an encouraging smile. "By the way, the giant told Inocencio and me that his name is 'El Diablo.' I think it is the perfect name for him, don't you?"

"The perfect name!" said Amelia and gave her one more quick hug. "I will call him El Diablo from now on. Thank you for your help and concern, señora. And do be very careful."

They walked around the tree and back toward the marketplace. As they approached the booth, Milly heard Leslie and Julia chatting busily in Spanish. Julia seemed to be showing Leslie how to weave, and they were laughing together at his clumsiness. Julia spoke to her mother in Zapotec, and Amelia joined the laughter. Then she switched back to Spanish for Milly's sake. And Leslie's.

"Julia says that while you and I were talking, señora, the American boy sold all my mantelitos to the other tourists. Julia says this boy plans to be a big businessman when he grows up, and he's getting his start here today."

Leslie said loudly, "I'm already a big businessman. I have proved it just now. Right here! Call on me any time you need help, Amelia."

Milly rolled her eyes. She put a hand on Leslie's shoulder to curb his bragging and to steady herself while she stood on one foot and rubbed her still-aching instep up and down the calf of her other leg. Too bad she couldn't sic this little juggernaut on El Diablo, she thought with a wry grin.

The ride home gave Milly an opportunity to re-appraise the now infamous El Diablo, and she wondered again about his relationship with Sánchez. It seemed fairly clear that they had been connected at one time, in spite of Sánchez' denial. If they'd been partners then, she reasoned, maybe they were partners still, and they'd had a temporary falling out. That would explain why Sánchez was going to such lengths to avoid the fellow.

Of course she could solve *her* problem by evicting Sánchez and his family from Casa Colonial. This seemed a wonderfully simple and effective maneuver until she asked herself what she would do if the Sánchez family refused to go. She couldn't physically carry them out the door and set them in the street, and she definitely could not rely on the Mexican courts and police to do the job for her. Anyway, she admitted regretfully, she didn't want to make an enemy of either Sánchez or his perhaps-partner, El Diablo. Who could tell what either of them might do?

Milly decided to talk it over with Inocencio before she made a move-—he was sensible and tough-—but for the moment, she resigned herself to a wait-and-see approach. If she could just hang in there for a few more days, the Sánchez family would go home to Mexico City. Right now she was tired, the road was bumpy, and she longed for a cold drink and a short rest before dinner. Soon she heard the horns and the stop-and-go sounds of city traffic, and at last the bus turned onto Calle Miguel Negrete and squealed to a stop in front of Casa Colonial. She glimpsed the green walls, heard the front door open and Inocencio's greeting.

"Welcome home."

"Thank you, Inocencio. Do we have water in the kitchen today?"

"Yes, we have water. There were no leaking faucets this morning."

"Good!" She brushed past him, calling back over her shoulder, "I need to discuss something with you later when you have the time." She walked down the orchid arbor and on through the garden to her cottage. It was sheer bliss to kick off her shoes, have a long drink of water from the carafe on the bedside table, and relax in her comfortable old rocking chair.

Right away there was a knock on her door. Could it be Inocencio so soon?

"*Pase,*" Milly called. She looked up, waiting to identify her caller, and heard Olga's hearty voice.

"Hello, Milly. I'm sorry I didn't feel like going vis you sis morning. Poul said you all had a vonderful time."

"I hope everyone enjoyed it. How are you feeling, Olga?"

"I am vell, sank you." She lowered her voice and spoke with exaggerated clarity. "I have somesing important to tell you, Milly."

Oh, dear. "Something important" was exactly what Amelia had said no more than an hour ago, and her news had been terrible. Milly waited, hoping that Olga's earth-shaking event was merely a hole in her bath towel.

"What is it, Olga?"

"Vhen I vas in se shower sis morning, vun of se men came in and looked at me."

Milly stopped rocking. In some confusion she ran through a quick mental list of the men in the house. They'd all been on the bus trip with her this morning.

Everyone but Sánchez.

"Who was it, Olga?"

"I don't know who it vas. I chust sought I should tell you about it."

"Do you mean it was some stranger?" Dear God, she thought, don't let it be El Diablo! "Was he a big man?"

"No," Olga said scornfully, "he vas liddle."

Milly squelched a giggle. At the same time she gave an inward sigh of relief. At least El Diablo hadn't been here. Actually she was shocked by Olga's revelation. Nothing like this had ever before happened at Casa Colonial. But she had to admit to a tiny kernel of prurient curiosity. "What did he do?" she asked.

"He didn't do anysing. He chust looked at me. I had finished vashing and vas standing qvietly viss se hot vater running over my shoulders. Se next sing I knew, some man jerked back se curtain. He valked out right avay, and I don't vear my eyeglasses in se shower, so I couldn't tell if it vas Inocencio or se gardener. But I sought you should know vhat goes on behind your back vhen you're not here. Sat's all!" She sounded huffy as hell, and Milly didn't blame her.

"I do understand, Olga, and I'll look into it. Thank you for telling me." Milly suspected that her reply sounded lame, but she didn't know what else to say.

Olga went out, the screen door slammed, and Milly began rocking again. Furiously. Who could the intruder have been? If this was one more sordid episode involving Sánchez, she'd *have* to find a way to get him out of her house.

She couldn't imagine either Elpidio or Inocencio being the least bit interested in peeping. Besides, neither of them would have the gall to march into a foreign woman's bathroom and strip back the shower curtain. She had to grin, though, as she pictured Inocencio staggering backward at the sight of a naked Valkyrie with steamy water coursing over her majestic boobs. At eye level, yet, for him!

Milly couldn't possibly ask him about it. He'd be insulted and she'd be embarrassed.

It had to be Sánchez.

CHAPTER 9

Half an hour later, Olga wore her new Yalálag cross to the dinner table, and everything hit the fan.

Milly, unable to see the cross, and thus unaware of the impending explosion, chatted amiably with Elmer about Oklahoma. She had lived there as a child and recalled it fondly. Elmer had just described working for Kerr McGee at a time some years ago after that company had dredged the Arkansas River to turn Tulsa into a thriving seaport.

At the other end of the table, Adriana and Yolanda were talking with Evelyn. Unexpectedly, Yolanda's voice slid up a full octave and splintered like ice on a winter pond. "Where did you get that cross, Olga?" she demanded in English.

"At Casa Victor. Isn't it lovely?"

Yolanda got up and stomped around to Olga's side of the table. "Yes, it's very lovely," she said nastily. "Give it to me."

"I beg your pardon?"

"I said give it to me. It's mine!"

"Sat's vhat I sought you said. No, don't touch it. Don't you dare touch it. It's not yours. I bought it and I paid for it. It belongs to *me*."

Yolanda's voice rose another notch. "My mother was

still negotiating the price when you stole it away from us. You're a thief!"

"Oh!" gasped Olga. "How can you say such a sing?"

"I can say it easily and I'll say it again: you're a fat old bitch and you're a *sief*, I mean *thief*!"

"Vhat a terrible sing to say!" whimpered Olga, and burst into tears.

Poul consoled her with a nervous "Sehre-sehre."

Elmer cleared his throat. "Jesus Christ, Milly," he grumbled, "What the hell's the matter with that Mexican shrew?"

"That's enough, Elmer," warned Billie Jo. "Stay out of it!"

Leslie's childish voice rose above the others, clear and pure as a spring breeze. "I'll lay three to one on the big Dane. Any takers?" George and Evelyn made no attempt to shush him. Perhaps they were too shocked to react.

Angrily, Milly racked her brain for a way to end the battle. "Doña Adriana," she ordered in her most severe, school-teacher voice, "control your daughter!"

Adriana obeyed. Perhaps she'd been schooled where nuns issued orders and students leapt to comply. "Yolanda," she said in Spanish, "sit down and behave yourself."

Milly heard the pounding of Yolanda's heels as she walked back around the table, heard her chair scrape the floor as she resumed her place beside her mother. "It's just not fair," she whined childishly.

Adriana interrupted her. "You have a choice, *mi hija*," she said, still in Spanish. "Either be quiet, or leave the room."

"But Mamá, you know that Papá said I could have the cross, and you promised...."

"You heard me, Yolanda!"

The younger woman jumped to her feet, knocking over her chair. "I hate all of you," she screamed in English, and fled, weeping, into the patio.

"I apologize for my daughter," said Adriana, and followed her out of the room.

Once again, the thirty-year-old Yolanda had behaved like a spoiled child. Milly shook her head in disbelief.

Everyone else went on with the meal in embarrassed silence. For a few moments, Milly could hear only the clink of knives and forks, the scrape of cups across saucers and an occasional snuffle from Olga.

She felt an urge to break the unnatural quiet. "Olga, you've had a terrible day so far. Are you okay? Things are bound to get better, you know."

Olga trumpeted into her hankerchief. Milly had never heard a nose blown with so much expression. It fairly resounded with outrage and obstinacy.

"Sank you, Milly. I'm fine. I chust von't vear se darned cross again until I get home."

Leslie urged, "Oh, go ahead and wear it! I'd like to see what happens next."

Milly fixed him with a beady eye. "What happens next, young man, is that you will behave yourself and display some respect for your elders."

"I will when they've earned it," was the surly reply, but Leslie muttered it in Spanish, and so softly that Milly pretended not to hear.

Cripes, she thought, *what an uproar!* Usually, she could draw a roomful of strangers together over the dinner table, but this bunch seemed ready to explode. She despaired of ever molding them into a friendly group.

Herbert's voice spoke in her mind. *They don't have to love each other, you know.*

No, she replied silently, *but they could be civil.*

She thought wistfully how pleasant it would be to eat three meals a day in peace and harmony. It wasn't too much to ask, was it?

Graciela served strawberry pie for dessert, which helped a whole lot to restore a pleasant atmosphere to the dining room. The local berries were small and dark red, with intense flavor. George had seconds and Billie Jo asked for the pie recipe. All the same, Milly was relieved when the meal had ended and she could escape to her cottage for a siesta.

An hour and a half later, she awoke to church bells chiming four o'clock. At the same time, she heard a knock on her door.

"Who is it?"

"It's Inocencio, señora. May I come in?"

"Yes, do come in."

She heard the door open and close, and Inocencio said, "I have asked my son Roberto, to bring his taxi. Would you like to go with me to pick out the new bath towels?"

"Yes, I'd like that. Where should we go?"

"I think the best place for towels is Sears." He gave it the Spanish pronunciation, "Say-arse," and Milly grinned to herself. She tossed aside her afghan and sat up on the side of the bed. She slipped her feet into her shoes and stood up, smoothing her skirt.

"I'll comb my hair and meet you at the front door in a minute or two," she said.

As she left the cottage and walked through the garden, she pondered on the best way to tell Inocencio about El Diablo and his one-man invasion of Santo Tomás Jalieza. She hoped that Inocencio, who had thirteen children of his own, would be able to think of a way for Paco and Amelia to protect their family. The idea of those children being in jeopardy was almost too terrible to contemplate.

It was not far to Say-arse. Roberto found a parking space where he could wait for them, and Milly and Inocencio entered the store.

"We won't be able to get the towels today," he warned.

"Why not?"

"They have only one of each kind here. You look over the samples, pick out what you want, and they'll order them from the warehouse in Mexico City."

Milly fingered the samples, feeling for the best quality. Inocencio just asked the clerk about prices. Milly knew that if she left it to him, he'd order whatever was cheapest, so she didn't ask his opinion. Three years ago he'd ordered towels so thin they'd felt like wet gauze. To Milly's embarrassment, one guest had written from New York to tell her that the Casa Colonial bath towels were worthy of rejection by a Bowery flophouse.

"These are the thickest," Milly said now. "They're the ones I want. Do they have them in yellow?"

"Yes, they have them in yellow."

"Okay, get forty-five bath towels and forty-five face towels of the best quality. In yellow."

"Do we really need those expensive towels? Wouldn't you rather get the medium-priced ones?" Inocencio sounded quite calm. It was as if he were resigned to her extravagance, but felt honor bound to at least mention thrift—to "give it the old college try," as Herbert would have said.

"No," Milly told him, "these are the ones I want. When it comes to sheets and towels, we should buy the very best quality. They may cost twice as much, but they last three times as long, so in the end they're cheaper."

Inocencio grunted, but he didn't argue. He placed the order with the clerk, wrote a check, and they left the store to find Roberto and the taxi.

"It will be suppertime soon," Milly said, "why don't we drop you off at your house and Roberto can take me home after that. There's something I need to talk to you about on the way."

"All right, señora."

As the car started moving she said, "You remember that huge man, El Diablo, don't you?"

"Ay-yi, I wish I could forget him!"

"Amelia says that he has murdered two people."

"What? Two murders? How does she know that?" His voice sounded disbelieving.

"Paco told her. He seems to know all about it. She believes Paco, and so do I. I think that big man is quite capable of murder."

"You're probably right. He's crude and very mean. I suspect that he's capable of almost anything. Come to think about it, I did hear some gossip about a corpse sitting on a bench at the bus stop near Santo Tomás, but I haven't heard a word about a second murder."

Milly was not surprised that Inocencio took the news of a double murder pretty much in stride. She had lived in Oaxaca long enough to know that any death was accepted here as an inevitable part of life. And she could always count on good old reliable Inocencio to cut through the emotional stuff and get right down to cases.

She said, "And now El Diablo is trying to force Paco to plant marijuana in his corn fields. If Paco doesn't do it, El Diablo says he'll harm their children."

"That is very bad!"

"What do you think Paco should do?"

Inocencio spoke firmly and without hesitation. "Paco should plant the marijuana."

Milly was thunderstruck. Inocencio was a law-abiding citizen, more honest than anyone she knew.

"Even if he's caught and goes to jail?"

"Yes, even if he's caught and goes to jail! Anyway," he added, "the chances are that Paco won't get caught because El Diablo will have paid the federales to shut their eyes to what he's doing. Those big drug guys pay off everyone; the chief of police, the mayor, even a brujo now and then! Look," he explained patiently, "it's simple: when children are threatened, their parents must do whatever is necessary to protect them."

Milly thought this over. She agreed with Inocencio. Up to a point.

"But if Paco gives in to pressure now," she said, "he'll be trapped forever. El Diablo will expect him to grow marijuana over and over. Eventually, he's bound to get caught."

"That may be," admitted Inocencio, "but for now, he should do what he's told. That will keep his children safe while giving him time to make a plan."

"Oh, yes, he certainly does need a plan! Think about it,

will you please? We should help him if at all possible."

"All right. We'll help him."

The car glided to a stop in front of Inocencio's house. "I'll talk about Paco's problem with my daughter," he said, "the one who's a lawyer in the district attorney's office. Between the two of us, maybe we'll think of a good idea."

He opened the door and got out, then just stood there on the sidewalk. Milly wondered what he was waiting for.

"After this," he said sternly, "you'd better tell me who is going with you on your bus trips and who is left behind. I need to know who is in the house at all times."

How did this relate to El Diablo? Milly wondered. Inocencio seemed to be talking about something very important, but she couldn't quite figure out what it was.

"All right," she replied evenly, and struggled to shift her mental gears to whatever was bothering him. His body language, from what she could see of him against the light, conveyed great tension, but when he spoke, his voice sparkled with mischief.

"By the way," he said, waving his arms in the air, his voice rising, "whoever that woman was in the shower this morning, tell her I'm going to the brujo and have her *erased from my memory!*" He slammed the door, smacked his open palm against the side of the car, and the taxi shot away from the curb and out into the stream of traffic.

Slowly, Milly caught his drift. This morning, after they had all left on the bus excursion to Santo Tomás, Inocencio must have made his rounds of the bathrooms, checking for leaky faucets. When he heard a shower running he was probably livid! With considerable delight, Milly imagined him scurrying into this bathroom, jerking back the shower curtain to turn off the faucet, and recoiling from a pink, steaming and outraged Olga.

She giggled, then clapped both hands over her mouth to keep from roaring with laughter.

Roberto probably thought she'd lost her marbles.

CHAPTER 10

Everyone came to supper except Rodolfo Sánchez, and everyone behaved in a civilized manner. Milly was relieved. She led the conversation by telling about her trip with Inocencio to buy the new bath towels.

Leslie, with a typical ten-year-old's delight in anatomical humor, laughed inordinately at "Say-arse."

"Did y'all order washcloths to match the towels?" asked Billie Jo.

"Well, no," confessed Milly. "It's so painful for Inocencio to spend money that I make occasional concessions for his peace of mind. Today's compromise is that he will make washcloths out of the old bath towels. I hope it works out all right."

"Hmm," said Elmer, "makin' washcloths is not a bad idea. Maybe we should do that at our house."

"Or maybe not!" Billie Jo muttered.

Poul said, "Inocencio must haf grown up in a poor family. Most people, if effer sey haf been wery poor, harbor a great fear of returning to powerty."

Milly nodded sympathetically. "Inocencio and Lidia did have thirteen children to provide for. Besides that, I think he finds it a heavy responsibility to run this place efficiently and take care of me, too. I tease him about being tight-fisted, but he is a wonderful manager."

"Have you ever been poor?" asked Leslie.

Elmer answered. "That's a personal question, son, but I can tell you that almost anyone who lived through the Great Depression knows what it's like to be poor."

Leslie ignored him. "I mean you, personally, Milly. Were you ever poor?"

What a persistent child, Milly thought to herself. He always sounds so aggressive. But this time she thought she heard the edge of anxiety in his voice.

"Well, let's see," she said, "I've never had to go hungry, but I came close to it a couple of times. Once when Herbert and I were first married, there was nothing in the house to eat and I had no money for groceries. I went down to the orchard to pick dandelion greens. Herbert borrowed his father's shotgun, let fly with both barrels into a flock of blackbirds and we had blackbird pie and dandelion greens for supper."

"Wow! How many birds did he get with one blast?"

"Exactly four-and-twenty!"

Leslie snickered. "When the pie was opened did the birds begin to sing?"

"Of course! To be truthful, I didn't even count the little buggers. Each bird turned out to be just one pitiful bite. They're terribly small when you take off all the feathers. And we had to chew carefully because they were full of shotgun pellets and we couldn't afford to go to the dentist if we broke a tooth."

Everyone laughed except Adriana and Yolanda. Milly noted that they were keeping an extremely low profile this evening. Either they were unable to relate to the concept of poverty, or they were still embarrassed by Yolanda's behavior over Olga's Yalálag cross. George and Evelyn were silent too. But then, they always seemed to rely on Leslie to carry the conversational ball.

"How about the people of Santo Tomás?" he asked. "Are Julia and her family poor?"

Ah, thought Milly, so this is what Leslie is concerned about.

"Yes, they're poor, but only by our standards. They own their land free and clear, their family is rock solid and so is their community. They're also part of a splendid culture that goes back nearly three thousand years, so in many ways they're rich."

"Do they have a car and a TV?"

"Nope, they can't even afford a washing machine."

"No TV? That's awful!"

"It seems awful to you, but everybody in their village is in the same financial boat. Somehow, when everyone is hard up, you don't resent poverty quite so much. Or at least that's how it seemed to my family during the depression."

"I hope Amelia and Julia and the others are okay," Leslie said, sounding worried. "I'd hate it if they were hungry and miserable." He paused, apparently thinking deeply. "I'm *never* going to be poor," he announced. "I'm going to work hard, invest brilliantly, and be as rich as a rock star!"

"Good luck!" said Milly. "If you can make bushels and bushels of money, you can use some of it to help people like Julia and her family."

"Yeah! I can do that. I'm gonna become a really rich, really cool dude!"

"Your parents can just relax, then," Milly said with a laugh, "and let you take care of them in their poverty-stricken old age."

George suddenly pushed back his chair, stood up, and left the room.

Oh, dear, thought Milly. Now what have I done? Well, supper was over, anyway. "Please excuse me," she said. "I'll see you all later."

She followed George out into the patio, intending to apologize for her *faux pas*, whatever it was. But once outside, she couldn't find him anywhere. It was getting rather dark so she walked all the way around the patio, turning on the outside lights as she went. No light was showing in George and Evelyn's room. She moved on through the garden, still wondering how she could have her foot in her mouth with no idea how it got there.

She passed her cottage, went along to the small patio just beyond it, turned on the light and sat down at the table. The evening air was lovely and comforting, like a warm caress, and heavy with the fragrance of night-blooming flowers. She lifted her face, closed her eyes and gave herself up to the serenity of the place.

It was very quiet. For the moment, not even a car was passing by in the street. She could hear voices from the dining room, faint and far away, as guests lingered over coffee. A stirring of the wind in the big jacaranda tree sent down a shower of seed pods. They struck the metal table in an irregular series of miniature crashes that sounded like corn popping in a pan. One pod dropped into her hair and she smiled and combed it away with her fingers.

As time passed, she began to feel as if she were spotlighted on a stage, there under the patio lamp with the dark garden around her. Where are the footlights? she wondered to herself in amusement, and squelched a ridiculous urge to stand up and take a bow.

A crackle of sound made her jump. She peered into the shadows, sensed movement there, and rubbed her eyes.

"George?" she called.

There was no answer.

Milly frowned. "Who's there?" She cocked her head, listening. She could make out only a rustle that might or might not be footsteps behind her, rounding the corner of room fifteen and passing into her vacant lot on the back side of the house.

Instantly, a paroxysm of hysterical barking came from the roof next door and Milly sagged with relief. Good old Apollo Thirteen had apparently spotted a cat and had gone into orbit. The cat must be what she'd heard in her garden just now.

Then a large hand dropped onto her shoulder and Milly herself came close to orbiting.

"Sorry I startled you," said George's voice.

"That's okay," she said, not meaning a word of it. Damned rubber soles, she thought to herself, I hate it when people sneak up on me like that.

"I heard you call me just now," said George, "and I thought I'd better come over and apologize for leaving the dining room so abruptly."

"Please don't worry about it. I hope you know that if I said something to upset you, it was strictly unintentional."

The chair next to hers scraped on the cement as George pulled it back from the table and sat down. From long experience Milly recognized the signs; she was about to hear some portion of George's Life Story. With patient resignation laced with a generous dollop of curiosity she waited for him to begin. She tried her best to look receptive and companionable.

George said, "It wasn't anything you did, Milly. You've been really nice to us ever since we got here. It was all that talk about being poor that got to me."

"Did you come from a poor background?"

"Yeah, dirt poor and the wrong side of the tracks. Fought my way up through the corporate ranks."

"That's not easy to accomplish."

"No, it isn't, but I did pretty well, actually. I have a big house and two BMWs, and I vacation at St. Moritz most winters."

"My word! Oaxaca must be quite a come-down from St. Moritz!"

"Oaxaca is wonderful. I love it here."

"But there's no skiing," she said with a small chuckle.

George did not laugh. "I told Leslie that we're here so he can practice his Spanish. But the truth is that we're traveling cheaply this year because I got fired. Downsized, they call it these days. I really should be at home, job hunting. I'm saddled with huge house and car payments, and my savings won't last much longer."

"I'm so sorry. Is Evelyn taking it well?"

"I haven't told her. We have enough troubles without my heaping a bunch of financial problems on her head."

"Your marriage is shaky?"

"We're not married. Oh, not that we don't want to be! But Leslie's father won't give Evelyn a divorce unless she gives him full custody of the child."

"Well *that's* not fair!"

"It's terrible! He's a high-powered attorney so I can't afford to fight him in court. He could drag it out forever and my lawyer's fees would eat me alive."

Milly was used to hearing confidences—people often told her their private business—but somehow this was different. I don't want to hear this, she thought to herself. I really don't want to know about it.

Aloud she said, "Leslie seems to love both his parents. Could he talk to his father and convince him that joint custody is what he needs?"

"That's what I keep telling Evelyn. She's a good mother and I believe she's in a stronger position with the court than she thinks she is, but she's afraid of losing her child."

"What's the father like?"

"I met him only once. He's arrogant, but he seems to want what's right for Leslie."

"Well, then..."

"At this point, the problem is Evelyn. Now she's decided that she wants complete custody. I'm afraid she's going to refuse to go back to California with me. I think she plans to stay here with Leslie and never go home."

No wonder Leslie had said they were running away that first morning in the dining room. His mother must be an idiot. Or perhaps desperate with fear.

Milly struggled to make her voice sound pleasant and non-judgmental. "Does Evelyn have money of her own? The only way for Leslie to receive an adequate education in Oaxaca is through a private school. How will she finance that? How can she pay for the idyllic existence she expects to have here?"

"She says she'll get a job."

"Number one," said Milly, "she can't work here legally unless she applies for citizenship, and that takes time. Number two, the minimum wage is about fifteen dollars a week. A *week*! A decent apartment runs at least one-fifty a month. I'm sorry, George, but I don't think it'll work."

"Then she'll expect me to foot the bill, and I can't do it. Only she doesn't know that yet."

Milly said quietly, "My, you have a problem, don't you."

She couldn't help thinking that, compared to Paco and Amelia, they hardly had a problem at all. Or at least the problem they did have was one they could resolve easily— if they wanted to badly enough—by Evelyn forgetting her own hurt and trying to do what was right for Leslie.

George said, "Leslie is Evelyn's child, so I have to let her make the decision herself, but I know from my own experience that it almost never helps to run away."

"No," echoed Milly, "it never helps to run away."

Later, as she lay in bed drifting off to sleep, she wondered what it would take to make Evelyn see the light. In her opinion, Evelyn should be back in California right now, concentrating on how to get along with her almost-ex-husband. It would make all their lives so much easier. Leslie's, especially.

Her thoughts naturally drifted to various American expatriates living in Oaxaca, including herself. Had she and Herbert been running away when they came here? she wondered. *He* might have been. *She* sure as hell wasn't. She had wanted to move from the family farm to a nearby town when he retired. She recalled the weeks of argument and the final decision, and she shook her head in resignation. Would she be better off at this moment if she were in some condo in Mason City, Iowa instead of here at Casa Colonial? Probably not, though she'd be lots closer to her family. That was her only real regret; leaving her family behind.

Hours later, she awoke to Apollo Thirteen barking furiously. "It-is-one-twenty-four-ayem," said her talking clock. Quite a long time after that, the dog sounded off again, even more loudly. Milly swore and touched the clock once more. "It-is-two-fifty-seven-ayem," reported the metallic voice.

She groaned and tried to go back to sleep. The damned dog had gone into his barking routine every single night this week, and always at about the same times. Some tomcat must have started prowling a regular route through her vacant lot. Maybe Elpidio could catch the little beast. First thing in the morning she'd ask him to set a trap.

Sounds like a whodunit, she thought as she drifted back to sleep: "Milly and the Case of The Meandering Mouser."

CHAPTER 11

Elpidio said, "Patrona, in order to catch the cat one must have a trap. To build a trap one needs the correct materials."

"What materials does one need, Elpidio?"

"One needs bamboo and nails, patrona. They are available at the *abastos* market."

"Muy bien, Elpidio. You and I will go to the abastos. We can buy groceries for the casa while we're there, and bamboo for the trap. It'll be fun. I've been missing our usual shopping trips, but lately I've been too busy to go."

Most days, Elpidio pushed Milly in her wheelchair to the big outdoor market. It wasn't that she couldn't walk that far, she told herself, but Oaxaca's sidewalks were uneven and she and Elpidio could make better time when she was on wheels. Besides, when she was afoot, nobody paid a lick of attention to her. But when she was in the wheelchair, for some reason she had never fathomed, the market people treated her with the kind of deference one usually reserves for royalty. She loved playing "Queen of Oaxaca" and thought it very funny to roll along, bestowing the royal wave upon her subjects from behind a lapful of cauliflower and chayote.

"I'll get my hat and gloves and meet you at the front door," she told Elpidio happily.

She hurried to her cottage, jammed a broad-brimmed straw hat on her head, gathered up her purse and gloves, then headed back across the garden at a snappy trot. Just as she turned under the orchid arbor, she heard the cochera screen door slam.

"Where are you going?" called Leslie.

"To the abastos market."

"Can I go with you?"

Milly took a deep breath and opened her mouth to say no. She didn't want today's outing complicated by having to keep track of this naughty child in the crowded market. On the other hand, she hated to sound like a cranky old lady.

She made her voice stern. "You may come with us," she said, "if you promise to stay close to Elpidio."

"I promise!"

"Then go and ask your mother. We'll wait for you at the front door."

Leslie was back in no time at all. "I can go," he reported excitedly.

As they set off down the street, Milly had to grin. What an odd assortment the three of them were; an old woman in a wheelchair, a brash American child and a young Zapotec in a straw sombrero.

As he had promised, Leslie stayed close to Elpidio and the two of them chattered away in Spanish. From where Milly sat she could hear only part of the conversation. It seemed to be mostly about how to build a cat trap.

"I can help with this," she heard Leslie say seriously. "I'm a Cub Scout and I have a book at home on how to trap wild animals without actually harming them."

"Why should we worry about harming this cat?" Elpidio inquired conversationally. "It's just a cat. Killing it by throwing stones would be very simple. Or perhaps I could shoot it cleanly with the pistola of the patrona's dead husband, may he rest in peace." He sounded hopeful.

Milly knew that Herbert's old pistol, which she had stashed in a suitcase on her closet shelf, held great fascination for Elpidio. In fact, he seemed to be on a perpetual search for situations in which he ought to use it. As usual, Milly ignored the hint.

Leslie said primly, "I believe that Doña Milly and I would prefer to build a trap."

Milly was surprised. To her mind, this humane approach to cat removal was a huge point in Leslie's favor.

Elpidio asked, "But what shall we do with this cat once we have caught it?"

"Hmm," pondered Leslie. "I know! I'll give it to my friend Julia who lives at Santo Tomás Jalieza, to have as a pet."

Milly rolled her eyes, but said nothing. She couldn't imagine Paco and Amelia accepting another mouth to feed, however small.

As the chair jolted across the railroad tracks all conversation was lost in the honking of horns and the roar of cars and buses tearing along the *periferico*, the broad street that encircled the city on its perimeter.

Elpidio seemed to be waiting for a lull in the traffic. "Vámonos!" he shouted joyfully, let's go, and took off, pushing the chair at a dead run.

Milly held onto the arm of the chair with one hand and her hat with the other. She hoped fervently that Leslie was sticking close. Elpidio stopped on the far side of the street, tipped the chair and ran it up onto the sidewalk.

"That was fun," Leslie said. He sounded out of breath.

Another half block and they plunged into the exciting and crowded world of the abastos market. To Milly, the very air was laden with commerce; she recognized the pungent odors of chiles, onions, cilantro, oregano, dried shrimp. Above the murmur of hundreds of voices she heard the thunk and grind of stainless steel drums revolving as they pulverized *cacao* beans, mixing them with sugar, almonds and cinnamon. For a moment all other odors gave way to chocolate, heavy and rich.

A man's voice shouted the traditional, "*Golpe!*" and Elpidio rolled her chair aside to make way for someone in a desperate hurry because he was heavily laden.

Herbert always used to say in wonder and admiration that everybody in Oaxaca was a capitalist. Here were thousands of people all buying and selling handcrafts, tools, furniture, foodstuffs, and God knew what else, just as they had done every Saturday for centuries. The only changes over the years seemed to be in technology and clothing. To Milly's mind, this place, supposedly the largest outdoor native market in the western hemisphere, was an astoundingly direct connection to Oaxaca's pre-Columbian glories.

The chair stopped and as the crowd swirled around them Milly felt someone place an object on her lap; a basket.

"What is this?" she asked.

"*Loritos*, señora," said a man's voice.

Milly slipped her fingers into the basket and found four warm, wriggling, naked baby parrots huddled together.

Leslie crowded close. "What ugly little things," he said. "They haven't any feathers at all and their eyes bug out."

"Are they not too young to leave their mother, señor?" Milly asked.

"No, señora. They are exactly the right age to bond with a person. If they stay too long with the mother, they will never learn to trust humans. Would you like to buy one, señora? These babies are very healthy and will grow into beautiful, green birds in just a few weeks. The price is reasonable."

"Let's get one," said Leslie.

Elpidio added wistfully, "Could we, patrona? I believe that Pepe is lonely and would enjoy having a friend." Pepe was the parrot already living in the Casa gardens.

Milly said, "I will buy a baby parrot, Elpidio, if you will

promise to take care of it." The moment the words were out of her mouth she knew she'd said a very silly thing. Graciela and Margarita would be stuck with feeding the baby bird; she knew it and Elpidio knew it.

"Señor," she said to the man, "when we have completed our shopping we'll pass this way again. If you are still here, we'll buy one of your loritos then. Adiós."

They pushed on through the crowd, down the long, long aisle to the very back of the market. Elpidio negotiated for the thin sticks of bamboo he needed, and when they moved on again, Milly held the bundle in front of her with the sharp ends on the footrest between her feet.

"Where do we find nails?" she asked.

"I've decided not to use nails, patrona. Inocencio has a ball of twine, and I'll tie the pieces of bamboo together. Don't worry, I know just how to do this. The trap will be very strong."

In the next aisle,` Elpidio stopped to haggle with a woman selling broccoli. Milly gave him her coin purse and waited for the bargain to be struck. Leslie's hand rested companionably on her shoulder. He was being remarkably docile this morning. She felt his hand tighten for an instant, as if he'd been startled.

"What is it?" she asked.

"I just noticed a small booth filled with weavings from Santo Tomás Jalieza."

"Do we know the weavers?"

"The woman looks kind of familiar, but I've never seen her husband before. Another man is facing them across the counter. I don't think they like him."

"Describe him to me."

"He's ab-so-lute-ly gargantuan and he has a black beard."

Oh-oh, thought Milly. "What kind of shoes is he wearing?"

"They're high-top sneakers with purple laces."

"I'd sure like to know what the three of them are

talking about, but I don't want that big man to see me. Turn the chair so that I'm facing away from him, will you please, Leslie?" She pulled her hat brim further down to shield her face.

Leslie turned the chair. "I'll stroll over there and listen," he said.

"No, Leslie! Don't go near that big fellow. He's a bad man."

"Don't worry, Milly. I'll be careful."

"Never mind about being careful, be *obedient*! You promised you'd stay close to Elpidio. Now do it!"

Leslie patted her shoulder. "I'll just try on belts and pretend I can't speak Spanish, but I'll hear every word. Then I'll come back and tell you what they were saying."

Before Milly could stop him, Leslie had moved off into the crowd. She had been wrong when she thought of him as docile; he was spoiled and willful! And dear God, how frightening it was to be responsible for a child who refused to obey. Where on earth was Elpidio? Why was he taking so long to buy the broccoli? If only she dared to get out of the chair and take charge of this situation herself, she thought in complete frustration.

By the time Elpidio got back, Milly was frantic. "Can you see Leslie?" she asked. "Where did he go? Is he safe?"

"I see him, patrona. He is buying a belt."

"Well bring him back here, Elpidio. The big man over there is the one who broke our hammock. He's a very bad person. I don't want him to see me, and I especially don't want him to know that Leslie can speak Spanish. When you go after the boy, please talk to him in English, only."

"But patrona, I can't *speak* English."

"All you have to say is, 'Come. Right now,' and then pull him away. Just get him out of there, Elpidio. Please."

Under his breath Elpidio tried out the new words. "Come! Ri'now!" He walked away still muttering to himself, practicing.

Milly sat alone, her head bowed and her fingers laced

together, the knuckles white. After a moment she heard Leslie protest loudly in his fluent Spanish and Elpidio say forcefully, "No, Leslie. Come. Ri'now."

When Leslie spoke next, it was almost in her ear. He sounded resentful. "Okay, I'm back! But darn it, you should have left me there a while longer. That big man was talking about planting marijuana. I think he's a crook."

"He *is* a crook!" said Milly. "That's why I told you to stay away from him. Now he has heard you speak Spanish and knows that you overheard what he was saying to those people. So let's get the heck out of here."

"But..."

"Andale, ándale, Elpidio! We'll talk about it later, when I'm sure he can't hear us." As Elpidio pushed the chair along she urged, "Faster, please. Run as fast as you possibly can."

"I can't go any faster, patrona. The aisles are narrow and crowded with people."

"The big man is coming behind us," reported Leslie in great excitement. "I think he's after me!"

Somewhere inside Milly's mind, Herbert's voice spoke loud and clear. *You blew it, Mildred. You drew attention to Leslie and Elpidio, and now you must find a way to keep them safe.*

"Turn off, Elpidio," Milly ordered. "Go left down the next aisle and find us a hiding place."

The chair made a sudden swerve to the left.

"Here are your friends the tomato vendors," said Elpidio. "Stand up, patrona. They'll take care of you and the boy. I'll hide with the chair."

Milly jumped to her feet. The bamboo clattered to the ground. She clamped her hand like a vise over Leslie's arm and walked forward, pulling him along with her. "Amigas," she said urgently to the women, "ask no questions, please, just hide us quickly."

A warm hand clasped hers and led her behind the counter. "Sit here, Doña Milly, and tell the American boy to crawl under the counter. It's draped with a sarape, so no one will be able to see him."

Milly didn't have to tell Leslie anything. He heard and for once, he obeyed. She sat down hard on what seemed to be an upturned wooden box. The tomato lady whipped the hat off Milly's head, put a rebozo around her shoulders and sat down beside her.

"Gracias, señorita," Milly whispered. She pulled the rebozo up over her hair and turned her face away from the passing crowd. Behind her she heard a metallic clunk and knew that Elpidio had folded the wheelchair to make it less conspicuous.

"Who are you hiding from, Doña Milly?"

"A very, very big man wih a black beard."

"I know just who you mean. I saw him earlier this morning. I don't see him anywhere now."

"Gracias a dios," Milly said fervently.

"Ay-yi, I was wrong. He's here. Keep very still, señora." The tomato lady stood up and moved to the counter at the front of her booth. "How may I serve you, señor? Our *tomates* are delicious and salubrious. How many would you like?"

"To hell with your rotten tomatoes."

The voice was deep, the manner rude. There was no doubt that this was the man who'd been looking for Sánchez at Casa Colonial and had been pestering Paco and his family; the man who'd supposedly killed two people. Milly gathered her borrowed rebozo closely, bent her back and turned away.

"I'm looking for the *viejita* who came by here in a wheelchair. Which way did she go?"

"No one like that has bought tomatoes here today, señor. I'm afraid I can't help you."

Milly felt a tug on her hand.

"I'm down here on the ground," whispered Leslie. "Get ready to run when I tell you to, Milly."

"Run?" said Milly in an outraged whisper. "Don't be silly. How the hell can I run?"

"I'll help you. Just be ready to move fast."

Milly was so angry that she had trouble holding her voice to a whisper. "I don't want to move fast, you miserable child. I just want to sit here quietly until that man goes away. Leslie, for God's sake don't do anything to rock the boat!"

But Leslie was gone again. Damn the child!

The big man let out a sudden bellow and fell across the counter. Milly jumped in surprise. She couldn't see him very well, but he seemed to stand up again and then fall to the ground, shouting obscenities. The counter landed on top of him.

"Come on, Milly!" cried Leslie.

She felt utterly bewildered, but at this point there was nothing for it: she stood up and allowed herself to be pulled along, around the end of the collapsed counter. The wheelchair clanged as Elpidio unfolded it. Leslie shoved her onto the seat, yanked down the footrests, and they took off at a mad run, Elpidio shouting "Golpe!" at the top of his lungs. They careened around corners, dodged back and forth across aisles, and finally rolled onto the sidewalk at the entrance to the market. Elpidio was breathing hard. His feet pounded on the pavement.

"Find a taxi," Milly ordered.

It was as if one had been waiting for them at the end of the sidewalk. Milly scrambled into the front seat. She heard the chair clang once more as Elpidio folded it, crammed it into the back seat and climbed in after it. Leslie crowded in with her.

"Casa Colonial!" she told the driver. Instantly, he gunned the motor and swerved into the stream of traffic on the periferico.

"Now," said Milly, "tell me what happened back there."

Leslie began to laugh. Milly wanted to throttle him. "I was hiding under the counter," he said, "and I could see that pair of huge feet right in front of me. I'm sorry, Milly, but I just couldn't help it. I tied those stupid purple shoelaces around the pole holding up the counter." Leslie dissolved into giggles. "When he tried to walk, he tripped and pulled the counter down. That was when I grabbed you and we got away."

"And that was when I lost my hat and purse and all the bamboo and the broccoli, and came away in that poor lady's rebozo. I'm so mad I could spit, Leslie. If you had obeyed me and stayed away from that man, he wouldn't have been chasing us. If you hadn't tied his feet to the pole, he would have walked away and we could have left peaceably in the other direction."

"But it was so much fun!"

"Fun?" she echoed furiously. "You broke your promise to stay with Elpidio, you were disobedient and you put us all in danger. I will never take you anywhere again. Never!"

They finished the ride in thundering silence. Milly felt that she hadn't gotten through to Leslie at all. He seemed happily convinced that life was a ball, that he was terribly clever and that he didn't have to listen to her because she was just a fusty old lady.

She was afraid to tell Leslie of the very real danger he'd placed them in and she didn't dare explain the big man's connection to Sánchez, nor to Paco and Amelia, for that matter. If Leslie knew too much and said the wrong thing at the wrong time, he could jeopardize the safety of everyone at Casa Colonial and the entire town of Santo Tomás Jalieza. Milly could only hope that El Diablo did not remember seeing her or Elpidio the morning he came to Casa Colonial and that he would not connect any of them with Rodolfo Sánchez. It seemed a very feeble hope.

At last the taxi pulled up to the front door of The Casa. Elpidio took the chair out of the back seat while Milly stomped inside to tell Inocencio that she'd left her purse at the market and he'd have to pay the driver. "Wait," cried Leslie, "we have to go back. You forgot to buy the baby parrot!"

CHAPTER 12

Poor Elpidio. Milly apologized for sending him all the way back to the market. Nevertheless, she told him he must return the borrowed rebozo to her friend, the tomato lady, right away, and pay for the damage to her booth.

"You're going to miss your siesta, Elpidio, and I'm sorry about that, but I want you to stay with those women until you have repaired their counter. After all, it came crashing down because they were helping us."

"Muy bien, patrona, whatever you say." Elpidio sounded long-suffering, but resigned.

"When you find my purse, Elpidio, please use the money in it to pay the lady for any damage we did and to buy a very large sack of tomatoes, and be sure to thank those women for their help. When you come home, remember to bring my hat and the broccoli. And of course the bamboo." Milly did not mention buying a parrot and Elpidio had sense enough not to wheedle.

After the excitement of the morning, Milly slept soundly during her own siesta. She awoke to the basilica bells striking four, and to the murmur of voices in the patio just outside her cottage.

"I have a cat at home," she heard Leslie say in Spanish.

"Her name is Cicely."

"Ceeceely," echoed Elpidio.

"Correcto."

"Does Ceeceely catch rats?"

"We don't have rats, but one morning I woke up and found a dead gopher on my bed. Cicely had brought it to me for a present."

"Was it your birthday?"

"Nope, no special occasion. I think it was just a little gift from the heart."

They both laughed.

Elpidio said, "Hold the bamboo like this, por favor, while I tie the pieces together...there."

"Elpidio, I'm afraid that if I let go of this, it will collapse. I think we should attach short pieces across the corners to make it stronger."

Milly shook her head and gave a cynical little smile. Leslie might give her a large pain in the Say-arse, but at least he was intelligent. She admitted grudgingly that somewhere inside his spoiled, untrustworthy little soul, there lurked a lively and engaging personality. She still seethed over his antics in the market this morning, but she wouldn't write him off completely. Not yet.

During her years of teaching she had learned that disobedient children could sometimes be the most interesting of all. It seemed to have something to do with imagination and initiative, and Leslie had plenty of both. She couldn't expect him to understand adult problems, for like all children his age he was the center of his own universe. She could only worry about what he might think of next!

She touched her clock. "It-is-four-eighteen-peeyem," said the mechanical voice; still too early to put on her hostess persona and visit with guests during the cocktail hour. For now, she'd just snuggle under her afghan and follow Satchel Paige's famous advice to "think cool thoughts."

THE DOG ON THE ROOF

No matter how hard she concentrated on pleasurable things, however, she found that she could not push the episode in the market out of her mind and she finally admitted that the chase scene with El Diablo had been her own fault. If she hadn't behaved so dramatically when Leslie described El Diablo, the child wouldn't have gone over to eavesdrop. And if she hadn't sent Elpidio after him...

What's the matter with me? she thought. *I never let myself brood about what's already happened or what might have been.*

Feeling guilty is counter productive, Herbert's kindly voice reassured her. *What's done is done.*

"That's right," she said aloud. "Leslie's a child and I'm an adult. I'll just have to make sure that neither of us screws up anything else."

Milly set her irritation with Leslie aside and turned her thoughts to Inocencio. He had promised that he and his daughter would figure out some way to help Paco's family, but so far there had been no suggestions. Maybe right now would be a good time to find him and ask if he'd thought of anything helpful.

She got up and combed her hair, tidied her clothes, and went out into the garden. She avoided Leslie and Elpidio and headed for the entryway, hoping to find Inocencio at his desk. He was not there. She walked slowly past the sala and down the other side of the patio. Not a soul was about.

Milly slowed even more, and as the specter of El Diablo invaded her consciousness once again, she felt helpless and a bit depressed. There was no escaping the fact that things were going haywire and solutions were still far beyond her reach. It was kind of like being a passenger on a speeding bus with defective brakes. For her peace of mind, she needed to gain some control over the frightening incidents that had popped up in her life these last few days.

Past the dining room, down three steps to the middle veranda, and she found herself in front of rooms seven and eight where the Sánchez family were staying. She dropped into one of the barrel-shaped leather chairs and stared morosely out into the garden.

She wondered idly where Sánchez was. She hadn't seen the man for a couple of days and no one had spoken of him. It was as if he had disappeared in a puff of cigar smoke. She remembered his cough and considered the possibility that he might be ill, although no one had mentioned it or sent for the doctor. She wondered what Sánchez did all day to amuse himself.

Several blocks away, she heard a diesel locomotive roll into the railway station, horn blaring. In the silence that followed, Milly heard someone crying nearby. She sat up straight and turned her head, listening. Promptly the weeping escalated to such wrenching sobs that she jumped to her feet in alarm. She followed the sound, arrived at the door of room seven and knocked gently.

"Are you all right?" she called.

The crying stopped.

"Please, may I come in?" she asked a little more loudly.

"I suppose so," said a muffled, female voice. It was hardly an exuberant welcome.

There was not much light in the room. Milly felt her way to the nearest twin bed and sat down on the end of it. She slid her hand along the bedspread until she found someone's foot. She patted the foot, wondering whether it belonged to Adriana or Yolanda.

"Are you okay?" she asked in a motherly way. "What can I do to help?"

"Nothing, Doña Milly. No one can help! My world is falling to pieces around me!"

This couldn't be Adriana. It had to be her overly-emotional daughter.

"Ah, Yolanda," Milly said, "Something terrible must be going on in your life. As my dear husband used to say, 'Nothing in this world is hopeless, because it *always* rains at least fifteen minutes before it's too late'."

"Whatever *that* means."

"Yes. Well. My husband sometimes said silly things that sounded sensible after one thought them over. And vice versa. Now let me guess what's troubling you. Hmm...I'll bet you're in love!"

"Yes, I am, señora." The voice quavered.

Milly considered this thirty-year-old "girl" and her overly-protective parents. "I can guess other things, too," she went on. "For example, I can guess that your parents don't approve of your young man. Am I right?"

"You are exactly right, señora. How do you know these things?"

"Because I've been there, my friend, both as a young woman and as a parent. One of life's verities," she added with a little laugh, "is that fathers never like the men their daughters fall in love with."

"I suppose you're right, señora." Yolanda sniffed dramatically. "Frankly, I think fathers are jealous."

"Yolanda, I'm sure your father loves you and wants only to protect you."

"That's true enough. At first, my father admired Ignacio for being a powerful man and skilled at his work. But a few days later they clashed, and now Papá has ordered me never to see my lover again."

Milly patted the foot and considered the word "lover" with some surprise. Did Yolanda use the term literally or merely to express a romantic notion?

"What did your father and Ignacio quarrel about?" she asked.

Yolanda's voice grew shrill. "How should I know? They ordered me to leave the room. I tried to listen at the door, but my mother pulled me away. I could hear the two men shouting at each other, but I couldn't hear their words."

"If you can contrive to talk with Ignacio again some time, maybe he'll tell you what it was all about."

"Oh, I still see him almost every day, but he refuses to discuss the quarrel."

Every day? Milly took this statement with a grain of salt. She had to wonder how the lovers could meet at all, let alone daily, with Yolanda's mother constantly hovering. Perhaps Adriana was a co-conspirator. Now *that* was an idea worth thinking about.

Milly said, "You might feel better if you were to develop a life of your own, apart from your parents; find a career, for example."

"A career? Pah!"

"Well, why not?"

"Listen. My father and I have been following the American stock market on his computer for many years. I have a real talent for choosing profitable stocks, but when I asked my father to give me actual money to invest, he laughed and patted me on the head. In his eyes, I am a mere child and not wise enough to be trusted. He'd never allow me to have a career."

Milly was a bit nonplussed. Sánchez hadn't mentioned anything about the stock market. Besides, investing in stocks and bonds had always seemed so mysterious to her that she tended to think of it as "playing the ponies."

Milly turned the conversation into an area where she felt more comfortable. "Have you ever thought of taking some courses at the university?" she asked.

"My parents will not allow me to even go near the university."

"I gather that your father doesn't believe in higher education for women."

"Both my parents believe in education for everyone, señora. My older brother graduated from MIT and my sister went to the University of Mexico."

"Then why not you?"

"My parents are afraid I'll be harmed."

To Milly's amazement, Yolanda's voice suddenly sounded flat and expressionless, as if she were withdrawing behind a protective wall.

"You see, my sister was murdered at the university. One

day when I went to visit her, I found her lying at the foot of the stairs in her dormitory. She was half-naked, bloody, and battered."

Milly flashed back to the day Sánchez had called Yolanda "our most precious jewel." No wonder. She was the only daughter they had left.

"I'm so terribly sorry!" Milly said gently. "What a devastating experience it must have been for you. Were you and your sister close?"

"Extremely close, Doña Milly. I was thirteen, and my sister was the one person in the world I felt I could really talk to."

"Pobrecita!" Poor little thing. Milly wasn't sure which sister she meant. Both, probably.

"One of my father's business rivals was convicted of the murder and sent to jail for life. But ever since the tragedy, for all these years my parents have hardly let me out of their sight. I understand their fears, but they smother me. I simply cannot spend the rest of my life under my mother's eye."

"What will you do?"

"I'm not sure yet, señora, but I think I have found a way to escape."

"How?"

Yolanda chuckled, sounding both sly and triumphant. Milly, startled, wished fervently that she could see the expression on her face.

"What I am doing is a secret, Doña Milly, but I guarantee that it will be an enormous—"

There was a loud knock on the door.

"Doña Milly," called Elpidio, "are you in there?"

"I'm here, Elpidio. What's the matter?"

"Leslie and I need you to tell us where to set the cat trap."

Milly felt a wave of frustration. She had been on the verge of finding out something terribly interesting; she just knew it! But Elpidio could never do anything without seeking her praise. Right now he didn't want her advice; he wanted her to admire his handiwork.

"Just a moment, Elpidio," she said crossly. But Yolanda had gone into the bathroom. Milly heard water splashing and knew she was washing her face, a clear signal that their conversation was over. Damn!

"I'm coming," she called wearily to Elpidio, and went out onto the veranda.

"It's here in the patio," yelled Leslie. "C'mon down."

Dejectedly, Milly went down the four steps to the small patio just outside her room. She took note that since awakening from her siesta, she had made a complete circle of the garden without accomplishing a thing that would help Paco and Amelia. Still irritated, she plunked herself onto a chair and Elpidio placed the trap on the table in front of her. The light was wrong and she couldn't see a damned thing.

"Very nice," she said curtly. "How does it work?"

Elpidio seemed not to notice her lack of enthusiasm. "It is a clever design, patrona. There is a door which is held up by this string. The other end of the string goes to the food, which is placed here, inside the trap. When the cat goes into the trap and eats the food, the string loosens and the door falls down, imprisoning the cat."

Milly warmed slightly. "The cat will fight to escape, Elpidio. Is the trap strong enough to hold it?"

"Sí, patrona, the trap is very strong. When the cat learns that it cannot escape, it will weep loudly in despair. But when it finally notices that the food is still there, it will grow calm and begin to eat again. This trap is like life itself, patrona: provided one has food, one can always manage to adjust to life's other problems."

Milly nodded in solemn agreement. Elpidio, though childish as ever, was having one of his flashes of perspicacity regarding the human condition. She wondered if he made up these gems, or if they were simply ingrained in the Zapotec culture.

"Go to the kitchen," she said with a smile, "and tell Graciela that I need a can of tuna. Have her open it and put the entire contents into a small dish. We might as well provide an extravagant feast for this very philosophical cat."

CHAPTER 13

It was time for lunch. Paco Soriano López unhitched his brother-in-law's team of oxen from the plow, clucked to them, and slapped the reins. Ponderously, the great, velvety beasts readjusted to the yoke and fell into step. With Paco and Amelia walking beside them, they made their dignified way along the edge of the cornfield and over to a patch of shade at the base of the cork oak tree.

All morning, Paco and the oxen had lumbered up and down the field, plowing under the stubble of the old crop and at the same time preparing ground for the new one. Amelia had followed behind, the hem of her apron gathered up in one hand to form a deep pocket. Over and over she had reached into the apron for a handful of corn. As she dropped each kernel into the groove made by the plow, she pushed a bit of earth over it with her bare foot and stepped directly onto the spot; kernel by kernel, one foot and then the other. The spacing of the new cornstalks would be determined by the length of Amelia's stride. Paco could give his full attention to the team and the plow, knowing that she'd do a perfect job. Over the years, through countless plantings, the two of them had perfected their slow, careful ballet. Today was a bit out of the ordinary, however: they skipped every third row and would return there later to plant the hated marijuana.

Paco felt lucky to have the use of these beautifully trained oxen, for many people had to plant their corn by poking holes in the earth with a stick. No one in Santo Tomás Jalieza had enough pesos to buy even one ox. But Diego, his brother-in-law, lived down the road in the village of San Martín Tilcajete where everyone carved fanciful wooden animals and had grown rich in the tourist trade during the last few years. Diego could well afford this excellent team that he had loaned to Paco for a share of the corn.

After they had fed and watered the oxen, Paco and Amelia settled down to their own lunch. It was pleasant there in the shade. Paco smiled and lifted his face to the light breeze. He took delight in the beauty of the countryside and listened to the sweet cooing of doves as they scratched in the dust and pecked at seeds among the grasses. Planting was a time of happiness and hope. Already he pictured lush cornstalks, fat, full ears and a plentiful harvest.

Amelia's worried voice jarred him from his daydream. "Paco," she said, "I've never planted marijuana before. How close together do you think I should place the seeds, and how deep?"

"I don't know, Amelia," Paco replied. He didn't want to think about marijuana right now.

"Perhaps it would be best to put two or three seeds into each hole, in case some of them do not sprout. Who would know how to do this, Paco? The brujo, perhaps? Or I guess we can always ask El Diablo, although I'd rather not."

Paco's heart seemed to freeze in the middle of his chest. "Why would we ask the devil?" he asked in a strangled voice.

To his amazement, Amelia laughed. "I'm talking about El Gigante," she explained. "I forgot to tell you that Doña Milly says the man we call 'El Gigante' actually calls himself 'El Diablo.' It seems to me that he should know his own name, so that's what I'm going to call him from now on. I think it suits him well."

Paco stared at the ground between his feet until his heart beat normally again. Why, he wondered, would the big man call himself such a terrible name? Perhaps he really was the devil. Grandfather had already reminded him that the devil frequently disguised himself as a mestizo who tempted men with the promise of money. Paco shuddered. He didn't want to talk about it or even think about it.

Amelia persisted. "My friend, Teresa, came over yesterday. She said that El Diablo told Enrique that he too must plant marijuana in his corn field."

Paco looked at her sharply. "I told you not to discuss that with anyone," he said. "It is dangerous. If some person in Santo Tomás tells some person in another town, word might spread to the federales who would then put us all in jail."

"I did not talk to Teresa," Amelia pointed out, "Teresa talked to me. She also told me that El Diablo has threatened Angelito Rojas and his brother Isidro and half a dozen other men. And those are just the ones she knows about. I suspect that everyone in town is involved and that El Diablo is menacing all of us."

Paco considered this idea with trepidation. Learning that El Diablo—he could no longer think of him by any other name—had such power over the entire village frightened him terribly. God help us all! he thought.

"God helps those who help themselves, Paco," Amelia said quietly.

Her remark had flowed so smoothly into his reflections that it seemed for a moment that he must have spoken aloud. Amelia managed to do this so often that he had almost ceased to wonder at it. He did not reply, but took a long drink of water and stretched out on his side with his back to her. One thing at a time, he told himself. Right now he'd have a short siesta. Later, much later, he'd think about the marijuana. After the corn was planted would be time enough for that.

Although he relaxed and closed his eyes, consciously striving for inner harmony, Paco was far from achieving it. His thoughts were inflamed. He felt angry at Amelia for reminding him of their problems and extremely disappointed in himself for not knowing how to solve them. Reluctantly, he sat up again and faced his wife.

"Amelia," he said, almost pleading, "I don't know how we can help ourselves. Does this mean that God has abandoned us?"

"Most assuredly not, my husband," Amelia said comfortingly. "I have no doubt that eventually, and with God's help, we'll be rid of that terrible man."

"I'd like it to happen soon, Amelia, preferably before we have to plant his accursed marijuana seeds."

"Yes, and also before he gobbles all the food in the village. Teresa says he drops in for supper whenever he feels like it and that he eats everything in the pot, just as he did at our house. It is the same with all the other families. Soon no one will have enough beans left to feed even the children."

"It would be against all custom to refuse him a meal."

"Of course. But it's a serious problem. I wonder if we could put something into his beans that would make him sick. I mean just sick enough that he wouldn't want to eat with us again."

"You serve the whole family from the same pot, Amelia. We'd all get sick."

"Not if I could put something into just his bowl, Paco." A calculating look crept across her face. Then she shrugged. "The trouble is that the only poison I know of is castor beans."

"But they're lethal, aren't they?"

"Yes, they are. Even two castor beans would probably kill him."

Two beans! They stared at each other.

The terrible idea swirled around them like a towering

thunderhead gathering momentum before the storm breaks. For the first time, Paco let go of the checkrein he'd been keeping on his true feelings about El Diablo. At once he was swept with such intense hatred for the man that he was terrified by the force of his own emotions. And as he looked into the eyes of his gentle Amelia, he knew that she too was struggling against the same wicked thoughts.

"No!" he whispered, "That would be murder!"

Amelia looked at him with frightened eyes. "God would surely refuse to help the village then, and you and I would go straight to hell."

Paco said slowly, "I'm afraid to go to hell. But I would make a bargain with the devil if I thought it would save our children and our village and our way of life." He looked down quickly, suffused with a guilty panic, wondering if he had spoken the truth. If the occasion should arise, could he really make that sacrifice? He felt sickened, confused by all this unaccustomed emotional turmoil.

Amelia said, "Paco, we have both been taught that it is wrong to kill. Even though it might seem to be the only course open to us at the moment, we must not do it."

Paco felt immense relief. "I agree," he said. "We'll have to think of some other way."

They sat in quiet misery, there on the hillside under the tree. Paco's head throbbed and he wished fervently that he had never heard of El Diablo and his marijuana.

At last, Amelia said, "I have an idea. If Teresa and I can convince every woman in the village to put castor beans into El Diablo's food, we can all do it at once. We'll be like an army making war on an enemy. If it is not an individual act, perhaps God will not consider us murderers."

"You're braver than I am, Amelia."

"You won't have to do anything, Paco. Just help me figure out a signal so that you and I will both know which bowl of beans has the poison in it at our house. I couldn't bear to live if we poisoned Grandfather or one of the children by mistake."

Ay-yi, thought Paco. He hadn't dreamed that deceit would be such a complicated business! They'd have to plan very carefully. Was it really worth the fear and guilt? he wondered. Then he thought about the corpse he and Amelia had been forced to bury in the dark of night only a few hundred yards from here. Even though the brujo had erased the memory, its dim outline lurked in the shadows of his mind. He thought of the sad young campesino slumped on the bench at the bus stop, a bullet hole in his forehead. He thought of the glittering black eyes and contemptuous sneer of the giant. And then he recalled little Julia on the giant's lap, trembling, her eyes imploring her father for help as she was held prisoner by El Diablo's enormous hands.

As if from far away, he heard his own voice say, "I'll do whatever is needed, Amelia. You can count on me." Madre de dios!—how could he have said that? Well, he was committed now and standing in the muck, so he'd better do it bravely.

Amelia said, "Teresa and I will see to it that every woman in Santo Tomás Jalieza is armed with castor beans, ground up and ready to be used, folded inside a piece of plastic and tucked into her belt. As El Diablo goes from house to house, every one of us will drop poison into his beans. When he dies and we are free at last, no one, not even God, will know whose castor beans killed him."

Paco shook his head. "To dig a grave big enough to hold The Devil will be very hard work and take a long, long time," he said.

He lay down again and closed his eyes, but now it was impossible to find any peace at all. He let his eyelids slide open and found himself staring at the tawny backside of Diego's ox. He gazed intently, using the prospect deliberately to crowd all other thoughts from his mind. He saw that the hide was quite beautiful, covered with a coat of short, silky hairs, velvety, like the cape of The Virgin in the church during Holy Week. When the animal moved, the coat rippled like dry grasses before the wind, shifting from brown to gold and grey and back again.

A shiny blue-black fly crawled over the mountainous rump. The ox flicked its tail and just in time the fly rose into the air a couple of inches. It hung there buzzing angrily for the merest instant, then settled back on the exact same place it had been before. Paco concentrated on the perfection of the fly's maneuver, admired its economy of movement.

When he was small, his grandfather had told him that they were all descended from the Old People, the ancient Zapotecs whose culture had survived through centuries of wars and invasions and was still intact. In the grand scheme of things, thought Paco, El Diablo amounted to no more than the flick of an oxtail. Once the big man was gone, the community, like the fly, would settle back into its exact same pattern of serene tradition.

Paco recalled tales of glorious battles against the invaders of the past. "You're right, Amelia," he said, "the women of Santo Tomás will rise up like an avenging army against the intruder."

"If the man calls himself El Diablo, perhaps he really is," said Amelia. "And if that is true, then God is sure to be on our side."

Paco rose to his feet. "Let's get back to work," he said. "While I'm plowing this afternoon I'll think about a way for us to identify the bowl of beans with the poison in it. I hope to solve that problem by the end of the day."

And I will, he promised himself. I must!

CHAPTER 14

The far end of the long, redwood table in the sala was Milly's special place. She came here so frequently to play solitaire that she had actually worn a groove in the table top. Solitaire, she claimed, was just distracting enough to allow her subconscious to take over solving the day's problems.

Today, as she carefully dealt the cards, she heard the door to the patio open. She smelled stale cigar smoke before she heard Sánchez' unmistakable wheezing cough.

"Buenas tardes, Don Rodolfo. I haven't seen you for a day or two. Are you well?"

"Buenas tardes, Doña Milly. I am very well, thank you. You haven't seen me because most of the time I've been reading in my room. Your library here at The Casa is filled with fascinating books." He sat down on the bench across the table from her.

"Have you discovered the large book about Dr. Alfonso Caso and his excavation of Monte Albán?" she asked. "It was given to me by the Caso family and it's one of my proudest possessions." She finished laying out the game. Her fingers searched out the braille bumps and she quickly memorized the locations of all the cards on the table.

"Dr. Caso was a truly remarkable man," Sánchez said in his flowery Spanish, "and the treasure found in Tomb Seven was magnificent. I've seen copies of that beautiful jewelry in the stores, but they were all gold plate. I've never found any in solid gold. Is such a thing available?" He stretched across the table, moved one of Milly's cards to another place, then turned up a new one.

Patiently Milly memorized the new card and searched out the location of the one he had just moved. She said, "There is a jeweler across the street from Santo Domingo Church who uses the lost wax process to make copies in eighteen karat gold. They are very expensive, but they're authentic." She figured that "expensive" was the right word to interest Sánchez. He'd probably send his wife and daughter to the shop immediately.

She turned up three cards, found a six of clubs on top, and moved it onto the seven of hearts that was already face up on the board. Briefly she felt the other cards to remind herself of what was there, then turned up three more cards.

Sánchez said, "Strangely enough, the book I have enjoyed reading most is *Sunset's Western Garden Book.* I had no idea that such sound advice about gardening was so readily available." He lifted Milly's top card, placed it elsewhere on the board and shifted yet another card onto it. Then he went back to the first stack and turned the top card face up.

Milly swallowed her ire and again passed her fingertips over all the cards. It was getting harder to remember them because of her irritation. It was damned rude of Sánchez to take over her game. Braille solitaire might be slow, but really! He must think she was a complete nitwit. Some day, she thought spitefully, she'd get someone to make her a set of braille cards without pictures on them. *That* would eliminate all the kibitzers.

"You're interested in gardening, then," she said sweetly. "Do you have an elaborate garden at your home in Mexico City?"

"No, señora, not elaborate, but quite beautiful, I think. I strive for serenity in my garden, and I try to use wide variations of color, shape and texture."

"Perhaps you could give Elpidio some lessons while you are here, señor. He knows very little. Any success he may have at growing things is pure luck. For example, one day he decided to transplant some snapdragons. They were three feet tall and in full bloom, and I told him they were too mature to transplant successfully. He did it anyway, by pulling them up, shaking the dirt off their roots, and sticking them back into the ground in another flower bed."

Sánchez laughed. "And they died, of course."

"No, somehow they thrived! This is why I say he succeeds at gardening by pure luck."

Milly turned up three new cards and waited. Sure enough, Sánchez played the top one and shifted around two more stacks. Resigned to defeat, Milly waited a decent interval and turned up three more cards. If she kept doing this, she thought in disgust, perhaps Sánchez would win the game for her.

"Has Elpidio ever planted marijuana?" he asked.

What?

"Not that I know of," she replied carefully. "He told me you mentioned this to him a few days ago. Why do you ask such a thing?"

"Because Elpidio is obviously talented, señora. Anyone who is both talented and lucky can usually make a great deal of money at whatever he does best."

"So you think Elpidio should plant marijuana in the Casa gardens."

"Well, perhaps not in the gardens, señora, although the plant does have very attractive foliage. But there is that long empty lot behind your house. What better place to plant a crop that will create a steady cash flow? I daresay you could make more money from your empty lot than you do from your hotel. The profits would be well worth the risk."

Milly wondered again if Sánchez could be a narcotics

agent trying to entrap her. She drew herself up, aiming to put an end to any such maneuver once and for all.

"Señor Rodolfo, do you really suppose that I can be lured into committing a felony simply by the mention of profits? Never, señor! I strive always to obey the law. Money is not that important to me, and it shouldn't be to you. Do you raise marijuana in *your* garden?"

"Certainly not, señora, and I apologize for suggesting such a thing."

He didn't sound contrite. In fact he seemed to find this whole conversation quite amusing.

"Furthermore," Milly went on, hammering the point home, "I wouldn't dream of corrupting Elpidio. He is a simple young man from the country and I am responsible for him while he works for me."

"Doña Milly!" Sánchez was now quite indignant. "I have already apologized to you once. That should be sufficient."

"Don't be snippy with me, señor! I'm the one who should be angry. On top of everything else, you know perfectly well that to make money from marijuana one must sell it to the kinds of people who carry *guns*! Clearly you do not have my best interests at heart."

Milly turned up three new cards, slammed them onto the table in front of her and glared at Sánchez as if daring him to touch them.

Sánchez grabbed them up and played all three, snapping them down with great vigor, one after the other. Then he chuckled indulgently and said, "My! You're a feisty little thing, aren't you."

Milly thought she might burst with anger. "You miserable creep!" she muttered in English. She was about to sweep all the cards onto the floor and stalk out of the room when the door opened again.

Elmer's earthy Oklahoma accent rang out. "Hello, Milly. Rudy, how are you? Where the hell y'been the last coupla days?"

"He's been reading all about gardening," Milly sneered.

"He's good at growing things." She could see Elmer silhouetted against the window. He sat down close to Sánchez, swung his feet over the bench and spun around to face her across the table. She gathered up the cards and sorted them, then shoved the deck aside and got halfway to her feet, ready to march out the door.

Elmer said, "Rudy, I hear you're lookin' for your partner. Have you found him yet?"

"Not yet," Sánchez replied.

Milly plopped back down on the bench. She hadn't known Sánchez could speak English, though she should have figured it out when he said he'd been reading the *Sunset Garden Book*. She was only a little embarrassed about calling him a creep—he deserved that! What caught her attention was Elmer's question about Sánchez' old partner El Diablo. How did Elmer know about *him*? She picked up the deck, shuffled the cards thoughtfully and began laying out another game. She was willing to put up with *two* kibitzers if she could hear something of importance. Her ears fairly twitched in anticipation.

"Maybe y'all should report this man to the police as a missing person," suggested Elmer.

"That's a terrible idea," replied Sánchez. "In Mexico, one does not contact the police. Not ever."

"Well, you can't do much from here, Rudy. Stayin' in this house all the time, you're pretty much out of the loop, aren't you?"

"I made a few phone calls before I left home. Now I'm waiting for my people here in Oaxaca to report in. I'll find him sooner or later." Sánchez rose abruptly, leaned across the table and played several more of Milly's cards. "Buena fortuna, señora," he murmured and patted her on the head.

Like a puppydog!

Milly's insides churned. Should she tell him off again? She had already set limits for Sánchez regarding the marijuana, but that was business. This was personal and he was a guest in her home. Dare she berate him about his personal misbehavior?

Herbert's calm voice counseled, *Patience, Mildred! Stirring manure only creates a stink. Remember, this guy thinks of head-patting as a gesture of affection. He even does it to his own daughter.*

Milly took a deep breath and forced her lips into a smile as she gazed up at the man. You patronizing sonofabitch, she thought. At the same time she tried to look as if she were grateful for his attention.

"See you later," said Sánchez and walked out of the room.

Milly fumbled with her cards, too angry to memorize them correctly. She turned up three from the deck and Elmer reached across the table to play one of them. She closed her eyes for a moment. When she opened them again she looked straight at him and asked bluntly, "Did you know Rodolfo Sánchez before you came here, Elmer?"

"I'm not sure, Milly. I b'lieve I might have had some business dealin's with him many years ago."

"What kinds of business dealings, if I'm not too nosy?"

"That's okay. To tell y' the truth, it's been so long that I can hardly remember."

"Try. It's important."

"Well, at that time I think he was exportin' stuff from Mexico to the U.S."

"What kind of stuff?"

"Gee, I forget—handcrafts, maybe? It was to come across the gulf from Veracruz, as I recall, then upriver to Tulsa. But I don't think my firm handled it for him. In the end, he must have gone through some other company."

"How did you know his partner was missing?"

"Billie Jo told me."

"How did she know?"

"I dunno. Adriana must've told her."

Milly nodded. She wasn't exactly satisfied with this answer, but it would have to do. At least for the time being.

With Elmer's help she finished up her solitaire game, then put the cards aside and strolled out into the garden.

Elmer stayed behind; to read for a while before supper, he said.

Pacing slowly up and down the paths seemed to help Milly think. She supposed that Sánchez *could* have been exporting Mexican handcrafts years ago, but it was hard to imagine him engaged in anything quite so innocuous.

Elmer, on the other hand, seemed forthright enough, and she was inclined to take him at face value. She had listened carefully and had heard no hint of deception in his voice. She could be dead wrong about this, of course. Elmer and Sánchez could be involved in a massive drug smuggling operation, for all she knew. But for now, she'd accept Elmer as he presented himself.

Sánchez had admitted to Elmer that he was looking for his missing partner. Then why had Sánchez hidden in the laundry the day that El Diablo came to Casa Colonial? She couldn't make sense of this at all unless...unless there was another partner she didn't know about.

Who could clear this up; Adriana, perhaps? Yolanda? Milly turned toward rooms seven and eight, determined to solve at least one small portion of the puzzle. She wasn't sure how any of this would help Paco and Amelia, but Sánchez had a definite connection to marijuana, so the more she found out, the better. And anything she found out about El Diablo could help keep her Casa safe.

She knocked on both doors, but no one answered. How disappointing. As she turned away, she heard Olga call from the other side of the patio.

"Yoo-hoo, Milly! Come and choin us."

Milly reluctantly shrugged off her private-eye persona and slipped into her hostess role. As she walked toward the sound of Olga's voice she could hear other women talking too, and she began to pick up the thread of their conversation.

"...and sere ve stood, vatching se parade go by."

Several people seemed to be seated around the table, and Milly could hear ice cubes tinkling. Billy Jo offered her a gin and tonic. Although she seldom drank, this time

Milly accepted. She sure was ready to take the edge off this day!

"What parade are you talking about?" she asked as she settled into a vacant chair.

"Sat's chust vhat I vas asking. Vhat vas sis parade?"

Yolanda's voice said, "Were they carrying a banner with gold fringe all around it?"

She and Olga must have made their peace, thank God!

"Ja. It vas a big sing on a tall pole."

Adriana's voice cut in. "Yolanda and I saw that procession too. We looked at the picture on the banner and decided that it must represent the butchers union."

"It couldn't haf been a political demonstration; se people looked too happy."

"Yeah," put in Billie Jo, "they were all smiling."

Milly said, "I doubt that it was political. It was probably religious. Every union in Oaxaca has a parade once a year. They choose a special day, find a band and march through the city to their church, carrying the official banner of their union."

"What? A religious butchers union?" giggled Evelyn.

Milly had to smile. Every woman in the house was here and spirits were high. This was a tremendous improvement over bickering at the dinner table. This was the way things were supposed to be.

"Vhy do sey do it?" asked Olga.

"To pay tribute to their church," said Adriana.

"I've been told that they're also giving thanks for a successful year," added Milly. "It's a lovely custom, I think."

"A lot better than going on strike," observed Yolanda, "although they do that, too, sometimes. By the way, Milly, I thought my mother and I had covered every shop while we were downtown today, but Papá tells me that we missed a fabulous jewelry store. Were you the one who told him about it?"

At the mere mention of Sánchez, Milly's disgust with the man returned full force. "Yes," she said gruffly, "I told him." She took a big gulp of her drink.

Yolanda giggled. "He told Mamá and me that you're a very lively little old lady. Did he by any chance pat you on the head?"

"Yes, dammit!"

"Well at least he didn't scratch you behind the ears." Yolanda raised her glass high. "Here's to my head-patting Papá," she said with a snicker.

Other glasses were lifted. Ice cubes plinked musically and laughter rang out. Milly listened with a degree of cynicism.

Olga's chortles quickly worked up to a burst of unfettered glee. To her, obviously, all males were lovable buffoons. She laughed heartily. "Men!" she spat in mock disgust.

"Amen!" cried Milly and sent a mental apology to Herbert, both for the sentiment and the pun.

She noticed that Evelyn's giggles sounded bitter. She must be thinking of her ex-husband. Yolanda could be laughing about her father *and* her ex-lover. With Billie Jo—who knew?—maybe it was just the gin. Even Adriana was having a chuckle at her husband's expense; something she'd never do to his face. Milly suspected that there wasn't much laughter in Adriana's life, in spite of her husband's doting indulgence.

"Tell me," Milly asked, "is it true that Don Rodolfo came here looking for his partner?"

"Yes, it's true," said Adriana.

"Are we talking about that big fellow with the beard?"

"No, Doña Milly, it's Rodolfo's brother Víctor, who's missing. He's short and always dresses well."

"His brother! That must be a great worry."

"Yes, Víctor and Rodolfo have worked together since they were teenagers. We're quite concerned about him."

"How long has Víctor been missing?"

"He came to Oaxaca on company business six weeks ago and we haven't heard from him since."

"I'm very sorry to hear that," said Milly. "I hope he's

okay and that you find him soon."

So she'd guessed correctly; there was a third partner. First thing tomorrow morning she'd ask Inocencio if he knew anything about Víctor Sánchez. It always seemed to her that Inocencio was related to half the people in Oaxaca and knew the other half. Maybe he could put out some feelers and locate the missing man.

Meanwhile, she'd say nothing to Adriana. No point in raising the family's hopes prematurely. How strange, though, that no one had mentioned this missing brother before now.

CHAPTER 15

The damned dog barked again in the night. Twice! Each time it sounded off, Milly listened in vain for the yowling of a cat. For some reason, their elegant, bamboo trap and its delectable bait were not attracting the wandering feline.

After a restless sleep, at last Milly became aware of morning light against her eyelids and heard the basilica bells chime seven. She showered, then fished through her closet for something snappy to wear, settling on a red and white blouse and navy slacks. There was just nothing like red-white-and-blue for good old-fashioned pizazz. As she was combing her hair, she heard a knock on the door.

"Patrona," called Elpidio, "I checked the trap."

Milly perked up. Maybe she'd been wrong. "Come in, Elpidio, and tell me all about it."

"Unfortunately, there is nothing to tell, patrona. The trap was undisturbed. Tonight I'll move it closer to the wall, and possibly we'll have better luck."

Milly felt disappointed; even a little desperate. She was fast approaching the point where she'd give almost anything for one lovely, long, uninterrupted night's sleep.

By the time she got over to the dining room, Graciela

was ringing the bell and the guests trooped in for breakfast.
Yolanda was late, as usual, but today Leslie was the last one
through the door. He came straight to Milly and stood
beside her chair, yawning and tucking in his shirttail. He
said, "Milly, I want to personally tell you how much I have
learned to love bolillos and hot chocolate for breakfast."

"Why, thank you, Leslie."

"But I have to admit that right now I'd give almost anything for a Pop Tart."

"Go on with you," Milly said, and aimed a playful swat
at his backside.

Leslie danced out of reach and headed for his place at
the table, laughing at her.

For a brief moment Milly allowed herself the luxury of
planning what she'd do to the child if he were hers and she
could get her hands on him. Then she turned her attention
to huevos rancheros.

After breakfast, she hurried out to the entryway looking
for Inocencio. He was not at his desk and this made her
unreasonably cross. Sleep deprivation, she admitted, was
ruining her disposition. She trudged back across the patio
and into the kitchen where she found him arguing with
Graciela over the day's menus. At times, Graciela was hard
to get along with, and today was obviously her day to be
aggressive.

"I don't *want* to cook pork spine today," she was saying.
"It takes a long time and the beans don't taste right when I
do them in the pressure cooker. I want to soak the beans
overnight and cook pork spine with beans tomorrow, slowly
and for a long time. *Ahorita*, right now I want to make roast
chicken with lime slices and brown sugar."

"We don't have any chickens," said Inocencio, "but we
do have pork spine. Cook it!"

"I don't care..."

Enough bickering, thought Milly. She said, "Graciela!
Soak the beans tonight and do the pork spine tomorrow.
But we're not going to special order any chickens, so forget

about that! Just take some hamburger out of the freezer and find my old recipe for 'Mexican Lasagne.' You haven't made it for ages. It may not be authentic Oaxacan food, but it's quick and easy and everybody always loves it. Put radishes, sliced tomatoes and broccoli vinaigrette on the plate with the lasagne and it will be an excellent meal."

"Oh, all right," was the sullen reply. "I'll boil some rice, too."

"No, don't," said Milly, re-asserting her authority, "it's not necessary. Serve French rolls with cilantro butter, instead. What do you suggest for dessert, Inocencio?" she asked, drawing him back into the decision making.

"I already made dessert," said Graciela.

"Well, what is it?"

"*Tuna* ice cream."

"Excellent!" Milly smiled to herself over the word "tuna," which was another linguistic incongruity, like Say-arse. Tuna was the fruit of the nopal cactus. Graciela used it to make a ruby-red sherbet that was tart and refreshing.

"Now then," said Milly, "I need to talk with you, Inocencio, but there's no hurry at all. Finish whatever you have to do, and come to my room when you have time to chat. I'll wait there for you."

Milly walked down the veranda and crossed the small patio to the cottage. She had solved at least one of the day's problems—dinner—and she felt better for it. While she was brushing her teeth, Ramona came in to make the bed and tidy up the room. The moment she left, there was a knock on the door.

"Come in," Milly called and settled into her comfortable old rocker, ready to talk with Inocencio.

To her surprise, Evelyn's voice said, "Hi, Milly. I came to ask you about something that has George and me completely baffled." She sat down in the other chair. "What *is* this thing?" she asked, and handed Milly a small piece of cloth.

Milly laid the cloth across her knee and smoothed it. It

was rectangular, barely longer and wider than her hand. It was hemmed on all sides, but the hems were bulky and the material rough. Interesting.

"I don't know what this is," she said. "Where did you get it?"

"We found it hanging on the towel rack in our bathroom."

"I've never seen anything like it."

The door opened again and Ramona said, "Con permiso, patrona, I need to put clean towels in your bathroom."

"Pase, Ramona. Oh—momentito, please." Milly held up the piece of cloth. "Can you tell me what this is?"

"Sí, patrona, it is a special cloth for washing one's face and body. Don Inocencio told me to put them in all the bathrooms."

"Of course! I should have seen immediately that it is a washcloth. Thank you, Ramona."

Milly managed to keep a straight face until Ramona had left the room. Then she grinned and held the cloth up by one corner with her thumb and forefinger. She spoke to Evelyn with exaggerated innocence. "Ramona says this is a washcloth. I wonder why we didn't recognize it."

There was a burst of surprised laughter. "A washcloth? Oh, yes, you told us that Inocencio was going to make washcloths out of the old towels. It's a lovely washcloth, but it's rather small, isn't it?"

"Small?" laughed Milly. "Why would you say that?" She turned her hand palm-up and put the cloth on top of it. Her hand was barely covered. "Why this is a perfectly adequate washcloth—provided you have very tiny hands and use only one hand at a time for washing your face."

Evelyn giggled. "Of course," she said. "I should have realized immediately that this very adequate washcloth merely requires a special technique for its use. You can hold seminars for your guests to teach them one-handed lavage—or two-fingered if they have extremely large hands—so that they won't lose track of this poor little cloth in one of those hard-to-reach places."

"Well," said Milly, "every cloud has a silver lining. At least we'll never have to worry about guests stealing them."

"Hmm." Evelyn pretended to ponder. "You might make a special rule about that—like if they take one washcloth, they have to take them all."

Laughing, Milly conceded that maybe Evelyn wasn't as foolish as George had made her out to be. At least she had enough snap to make a joke.

"Seriously, Milly, what will you do about these funny little rags?"

"Seriously? Not a damned thing. Inocencio's feelings are a lot more important to me than having Wonderful Washcloths. People will just have to put up with them."

"It must be fun to work for you," said Evelyn. "How about giving me a job? I could fill in on the women's days off. I know how to clean house and I'm a pretty good cook."

"I'll bet you'd be a terrific employee, but I doubt that you'd be willing to work your tail off for fifteen dollars a week. That's the standard wage in Oaxaca."

"Fifteen dollars! My gosh, that's really discouraging. I was hoping to stay here with Leslie for the rest of the year, but maybe I can't afford to."

"Not unless you have some other source of income. Anyway, you don't want to take Leslie out of school, do you?"

"I guess not. Not really. Oh, dear—the problem is that I'm terribly worried about going home. Leslie's father claims that the moment we get back to California, the court will take Leslie away from me forever. I don't know what to do. I really panic at the idea of losing him!"

"That would be awful," agreed Milly, "but Evelyn, you must know that it's not going to happen. No court would take Leslie away from you. You're a good mother and Leslie obviously loves you. He's fond of George too."

Evelyn sniffled. "I don't want to have to share Leslie

with someone who hates me and who lives so far away. I want my little boy with me all the time. My ex is mean and vindictive and tells Leslie lies about me. I want full custody of my child!"

"Of course you do," soothed Milly, "but for Leslie's sake, I think you should make a huge effort to reconcile with your husband—oh, not entirely," she amended hastily, as Evelyn sputtered, "just enough to secure his cooperation about joint custody."

"I can't possibly do that!"

"I think you're a big enough person to control your feelings for the sake of your child. Leslie loves both his parents, you know, and he deserves to have both of you in his life. Surely your husband has *some* redeeming features—after all, you chose to marry him." She gritted her teeth and added, "Leslie is a rather, uh...remarkable...child and he deserves a wonderful life." Well, Milly admitted to herself, Leslie could become remarkable, with a little tough love from his mother.

"Milly, I appreciate your interest, but there's just no way I could make peace with Leslie's father. He's utterly impossible."

"He must have changed a lot since you first knew him."

"Yes. A lot. I can't talk to him at all."

"Then have Leslie act as intermediary. From what the boy tells me, I think he and his father are close, and his father will do almost anything for him."

"That's probably true," Evelyn admitted.

"Then it's worth a try, isn't it?"

Evelyn left and Milly leaned her head against the back of the chair. She felt drained. She hoped her suggestions had lodged in Evelyn's sub-conscious where, with a little luck, they might germinate. It was really all she could do. She rocked slowly, gradually relaxing to the soothing rhythm.

By the time Elpidio came around with the wheelchair to take her to the market, she was feeling considerably more mellow. She wasn't exactly overflowing with energy, but knew that if she stayed home she'd probably just take a nap. Milly loved afternoon siestas, but drew the line at morning naps. Anyway, the trip would probably be worth the effort, for the market was endlessly entertaining.

Today, as they entered the market a woman from the country offered to sell her some fried grasshoppers.

"No, thank you," Milly said politely.

"But señora, it is a known fact that if you eat a grasshopper, you will be sure to return to Oaxaca."

"Thank you, señorita. I'm pleased that you want me to come again, but eating a grasshopper is unnecessary because I already live here."

"But they are also tasty, señora; crisp and salty."

"I know, and they are especially delicious with *mezcal*. Well, perhaps we should buy a few, Elpidio."

He made the transaction and put a piece of newspaper in her lap. The crunchy grasshoppers were folded inside.

After that, she had a quick visit with her friends the tomato ladies who greeted her with warm enthusiasm. She gave them the grasshoppers as a small gift.

"Where is the American boy?" they wanted to know. "The trick he played on the gigante was very funny. Everyone in the market has heard about it."

Milly rolled her eyes heavenward. "The boy was so naughty that day that I will never take him anywhere again."

"But we would like to see him, señora! The entire market is grateful to the child for driving away the gigante—who has not been back, gracias a Dios! That man is a brute, and we all hope we've seen the last of him."

Milly could well understand that sentiment. She felt exactly the same way. She had mixed feelings about Leslie's fame here in the market, however, since it arose from his naughtiness.

Elpidio strolled along, pushing her chair from one

booth to another. In addition to the items on Inocencio's list, they bought a couple of gorgeous eggplants and some especially large pecans. By the time they got home, it was almost the dinner hour.

The Mexican Lasagne was a huge success, as Milly had known it would be, and the tuna sherbet was a perfect ending to the meal.

As the guests lingered over coffee, Milly had a brainstorm. "I think it's time for another bus trip," she said. "How would you all like to go to a wood-carving village tomorrow?"

"You mean where they make those wooden animals that are painted so vividly?" asked Billie Jo.

Milly nodded. "There are actually three wood-carving villages, but I thought San Martín Tilcajete would be the most fun. It's a very small place with some excellent carvers who work out of their homes."

"Yeah," said Leslie, "let's go."

"Good. I'll have Inocencio make the arrangements, and we'll leave right after breakfast tomorrow morning."

And then it was siesta time, thank God. Milly sat on the edge of her her bed and had just taken off her shoes when there was a knock on her door.

"Pase," she called wearily.

"It's me, señora," called Inocencio. "You said you wanted to talk to me."

As the door opened, she heard a sound like a truck rumbling down the street, and when Inocencio dropped into a chair, the building shook. That's strange, she thought, Inocencio doesn't weigh enough to shake an adobe building. No one does.

"Earthquake!" cried Inocencio, bounding to his feet. "Come outside." He grabbed her hand and they staggered through the doorway into the garden. By then, of course, it was all over and they were laughing at each other.

"You'd think by this time we'd be used to those silly little tremors," said Milly. "I don't think anyone else in the house even noticed this one."

Minuscule earthquakes were common in Oaxaca. Milly knew that most epicenters were somewhere off the Isthmus of Tehuantepec and far out to sea. By the time the vibrations rolled up from the ocean floor and over the mountains to the Valley of Oaxaca, they were spent and seemed only a jiggly reminder that the gods of the underworld occasionally stirred in their sleep. Still, she had heard the disturbing stories of the 1931 quake that had leveled a good part of the city, but had not caused even a crack in the walls of Casa Colonial.

"Let's go back inside," she said. "There are some things we need to talk about."

Inocencio held the door for her and Milly sat down in her rocking chair.

"First of all," she said, "tell me if you and your daughter have thought of a way to help Paco and Amelia."

"We talked about it."

"And...?"

"I don't know of anything we can do unless they ask us to help them."

How exasperating! Inocencio's attitude was what she called the Oaxaca Catch-22 Syndrome. Offering help without being asked for it simply wasn't done; in fact, it was a definite social error. But no person ever asked for help because asking would make him appear incompetent. The result was a lot of aimless messing about while everyone politely looked the other way. Like Elpidio and Leslie building the cat trap by-guess-and-by-God. Inocencio probably knew about that project—after all, he had supplied the twine to tie it together—but he had never once mentioned it. He must be ignoring their efforts because they hadn't asked for his advice.

She couldn't resist probing. "Did you see the trap Elpidio and the little boy set in the vacant lot last night?"

Inocencio gave a snort of laughter. "I saw it. What do they expect to catch, an elephant?"

"A cat."

"Why?"

"Because I asked them to. The dog next door wakes me up every night by barking at some cat. They're going to catch the cat so I can get a good night's sleep."

Inocencio grunted. "As long as Elpidio does his regular work, I don't care how much of his own time he spends foolishly."

Milly's eyebrows shot up in surprise at his tone of voice. Cultural differences were so interesting. Coming as she did from a friendly, nosy, Iowa farm area, it was hard for her to accept a custom that seemed to prevent people from helping each other voluntarily when help was needed. She pushed the thought aside and turned to the problem foremost in her mind.

"What I really wanted to talk to you about is Rodolfo Sánchez' brother Victor."

"I've never heard of any Victor Sánchez. Who told you about him?"

"Rodolfo's wife, Adriana. She said that Victor and Rodolfo have been business partners for most of their lives. Victor came to Oaxaca on company business six weeks ago, and poof—he disappeared. They're here looking for him."

"What kind of business are the brothers in?"

"She didn't tell me, but I'm convinced that El Diablo is a third partner and that the company deals in marijuana."

"Señora, that's a rather wild assumption. How can you be so sure?"

"I have no solid proof, but Rodolfo told me that El Diablo was once his partner. Now you and I both know that El Diablo is forcing Paco to plant marijuana. Besides that, Rodolfo suggested that we plant marijuana in the lot behind The Casa."

"What? The man must be loco. We can't do that!"

"Of course not. I told him to mind his own business, and he laughed as if he were having a rude joke at my expense."

"Hmm. Dealing marijuana is a dangerous line of work

involving some very nasty people. Maybe Victor Sánchez disappeared because someone killed him. His family may never see him again. In fact, they might not even find his body."

"Oh, dear," said Milly, "I have a sinking feeling that you're probably right." She paused, thinking hard. "Do you remember that Paco told Amelia that El Diablo killed two men?"

"Yes, I remember."

"Well, one of them was the corpse left at the Santo Tomás bus stop. That one was identified as a local farmer. But the other one hasn't been found yet; we just have Paco's word for its existence. I suspect that this other victim could have been Victor Sánchez, but if that is true, where is his body?"

"God only knows, señora. He could have been buried anywhere out in the hills. I haven't heard one word of gossip about a second murder. And I have never heard the name 'Victor Sánchez' until this very moment."

"Is it possible for you to contact people in the other hotels, Inocencio, and ask if a Victor Sánchez has registered at any of them in the last six or seven weeks?"

"Yes, I can do that."

"It will mean extra work for you, and I'm sorry about that, but it's worth a try, I think. It would be awfully nice to find Victor Sánchez somewhere, preferably alive and kicking."

CHAPTER 16

By late afternoon, Paco and Amelia had finished putting in the last of the corn and the empty rows had been readied for the marijuana. Paco knew that now he would have to decide how to plant the detested stuff whether he wanted to or not.

He unhooked the oxen from the plow. The great beasts plodded slowly homeward with Paco and Amelia walking beside them.

"One time I saw some marijuana growing wild by the river," said Paco. "Each plant was quite tall and much bushier than a cornstalk, so I think we should place the marijuana seeds farther apart than we do the kernels of corn."

Amelia didn't answer. She turned away and trotted up and down the edge of the field, counting the rows as she went. When she returned and had fallen into step with Paco again she said breathlessly, "There are forty-two rows waiting for the marijuana. If we divide the seeds into forty-two equal piles, we can then count the seeds in one pile and figure out exactly how many to plant in each row."

"Have you looked at those seeds, Amelia? They are very small. I think there will be several hundred to each row."

"If it turns out that there are more seeds than we need, I'll just plant them anyway, Paco. We can keep pulling up seedlings, pretending to thin them, until we know that El Diablo is dead. Once he is gone, we can get rid of all the marijuana and plant corn in those rows."

Paco looked to the mountains, seeking reassurance. They seemed indifferent to his misery. "I'll leave all that to you," he said finally. "Start first thing in the morning and do whatever you think best. While you're planting the marijuana I'll return the oxen to Diego at San Martín Tilcajete, but I'll hurry home to help you. Maybe we can get it all done in one day."

"Muy bien, Paco. Somehow I'll figure out the right way to do it." After a moment, Amelia said, "Yesterday you told me to tear El Diablo's tortilla in half and put it on top of his food to signal that it's poisonous. That's a good, clear signal, Paco. But I've been wondering if it might be better to give El Diablo two tortillas, and everybody else one. That way it will appear that we consider him an honored guest."

Paco thought over her suggestion carefully. "I agree," he said. "Two tortillas. Do you think we should tell Grandfather and the children what we're doing?"

"I've been wondering about that," said Amelia. "I'm afraid the children would act nervous if they knew, but it would be a good idea to tell Grandfather. He's very smart and we might need his help."

Paco asked suddenly, "What does a castor bean taste like?"

"No one knows, Paco. Anybody who ever ate one is dead and can't describe it. But just in case it tastes bad, I'll put lots of extra chile peppers into the bean pot as soon as El Diablo appears. That should disguise any odd flavors."

They passed the end of the cornfield and came to Paco's small patch of castor beans. He turned to stare at the tall plants, and the oxen stopped of their own accord, swinging their great heads as if sensing his preoccupation.

Amelia reached high to pull down one of the rangy branches. The leaves were huge, a foot or more across, with large, pointed lobes. The beans grew in a cluster at the top of their own stalk, each one protected by a prickly husk. She selected two and broke them off, releasing the branch to spring back to its former height. She peeled away the husks and displayed the two beans to Paco on the palm of her hand. They were smooth, silvery, streaked with rosy red.

"They are so beautiful," whispered Paco.

Amelia pulled a piece of folded blue plastic out of her belt and spread it on a flat rock. Paco watched in horrified admiration as she found another rock and used it to pound the two seeds. When they were mashed to a pulp, she threw the rock away, folded the plastic without touching its contents and slipped it back under her belt. He noticed that the belt was an old one that she had woven many years ago; wide, faded black with a pattern in dark red.

Amelia stood up and turned to face him, her expression solemn. "I'm ready," she said. "Let's go home."

The boys had heard them coming and had opened the gate wide. Paco took the oxen around the house to tether them near the back wall—not too close to the pile of corn—and to give them food and water. As he rejoined the family he saw Julia stir the beans. Amelia had set them to soak early this morning, and Julia must have started cooking them the moment she came in from school.

Paco stopped at the basin by the door to wash away the day's grime, then approached his father who sat on his chair under the copal tree. Paco squatted close beside him.

"Did you finish with the corn today, mi hijo?" asked the grandfather.

"The corn is planted, Father," replied Paco. "Tomorrow those other seeds go into the ground."

"I know," his father said softly. "It is a great pity, but it must be done. Have you seen El Diablo, my son? Today is Thursday and he said he'd be back today."

139

Paco glanced around to make sure the children were not close enough to hear him. "I must tell you a secret," he said. "The women of Santo Tomás are going to poison El Diablo with castor beans."

Grandfather frowned and drew back a little. "You have to be joking," he said.

"This is a very serious matter, Father. I would never joke about such a thing. At this very moment Amelia has two crushed castor beans ready to drop into the giant's bowl. So does every other woman in town."

"Has the whole village gone crazy?"

"Perhaps we have, but it cannot be stopped now. What you need to know, Father, is that Amelia will signal which bowl has the castor beans in it so there can be no mistakes."

"God help us," said Grandfather, and crossed himself.

"When you see a bowl of beans with two tortillas on it, you'll know that the poison is in that bowl. El Diablo will get two tortillas. The rest of us will get one." Paco looked into his father's eyes to make sure he understood, but the old man was staring past him toward the gate. Paco glanced over his shoulder and saw El Diablo stroll into view. Don Porfirio, the brujo, was right behind him, his bag of magic slung over his shoulder, as usual, his expression stern.

The giant boomed playfully, "Buenas tardes, mi amigo Paquito."

Paco winced. "Remember," he whispered to his father, "two tortillas!"

Julia tapped him on the shoulder and whispered, "El Diablo is here, Father, should we run away?"

"Not this time, mi hija," said Paco, "not unless I tell you to. But if I do say 'run,' then you must take your brothers and run very fast." Julia nodded. Satisfied that she understood, Paco rose to confront their tormenter.

"Muy buenas tardes, señor," he said courteously to the giant, a very good afternoon to you.

140

"I dropped by for supper, Paquito, so we can celebrate the planting of the seeds I gave you. They are in the ground, are they not?"

"Not yet, señor. Today we finished the corn. Tomorrow we plant your magical seeds from which, undoubtedly, we will all make a great fortune." Try as he might, Paco could not keep the sarcasm out of his voice.

Don Porfirio stepped forward. He was a handsome old man, but rigid and humorless; kindly, but very conscious of his mystique and his position in the community. "Buenas tardes, Paco," he said imperiously. "I am glad to see that all is well with you and yours. I've had my supper, so don't worry about stretching the caldo de pollo negro. I'll just chat with the grandfather for a few minutes."

Out of the corner of his eye Paco saw Amelia drop several chiles into the bean pot and give it a stir. The family's mouths and bellies would be on fire tonight! But well worth it, he thought, if chile could disguise the taste of castor beans. They'd know about that soon enough.

Amelia ladled beans into a bowl, put one large, crisp tortilla over it and murmured to Julia, "This is for Grandfather."

Julia carried the bowl carefully with both hands and gave it to the old man.

Grandfather stared at it for a long moment, then turned to El Diablo and said, "As our guest, you should be served first, señor." He held out the bowl.

What? thought Paco. *What are you doing, Father? Were you not listening to my instructions?*

El Diablo took the bowl and turned to Paco with a nasty chuckle. "Paquito, you have worked hard today. You should be given food ahead of all of us. These beans are yours."

Did El Diablo suspect something? Paco tried to look pleasant as he held up both hands palm outward. He replied, as convention dictated, "No, no, señor, you are the honored guest."

"I insist, Paquito."

There was nothing for it. Paco shrugged and accepted the beans. Again he looked carefully at the bowl. One tortilla.

His heart pounded and he could hardly breathe. He knew he should distract everyone so that Amelia could use the poison when she was ready. He felt paralyzed, like the rabbit cornered by the coyote in the old Zapotec folk tales. But in those stories, he reminded himself, the rabbit always wins, so use your brain, Paco. *Think!*

He tore a piece off the tortilla and scooped up a mouthful of beans. "Hooh," he said, "those beans are hot!" He smiled and smacked his lips. He stepped closer to El Diablo and a little bit to one side so the man would have to turn away from Amelia to talk to him.

Paco said, "Tell me, please, how far apart should I plant the magic seeds you gave me."

"Paquito, that is a stupid question. Plant them every four inches and pull up the seedlings that do not grow well. What's left will be a vigorous crop. Any farmer should be able to figure that out!"

Julia brought another bowl, balancing carefully so as not to spill it. She looked from El Diablo to Grandfather and back again. The giant smiled and his eyes glittered. He gestured grandly for the older man to go first. Grandfather accepted with a gracious nod.

One tortilla.

Paco began to sweat. He couldn't tell if it was from fear or from the hot chile peppers. All he knew was that it was against tradition to serve women and children ahead of the men, so Amelia had run out of options. The next bowl of beans had to go to El Diablo.

He took a deep, steadying breath. "About how long does it take a marijuana plant to grow to maturity, señor?" he asked.

"Marijuana grows at about the same rate as corn, Paquito. Obviously, that's why we plant them together." El Diablo whirled suddenly and stared at Amelia. "Where are my beans?" he demanded, and watched her closely as she dipped into the pot.

There was a rumbling sound and the earth shifted. El Diablo took a step forward and fell to one knee. Everyone else stood still and waited for the ground to stop shimmying beneath their feet. Time seemed to extend, dreamlike, for Paco, even though he knew that only a few seconds were actually passing. He saw El Diablo on the ground, facing Amelia, saw her turn her back ever so slowly as she fumbled to draw the packet from under her belt. Paco took two sluggish steps, as if he were walking in deep sand, placing himself between El Diablo and Amelia to block the giant's view.

He said to El Diablo, "Steady, señor, it will be over in a moment."

Don Porfirio placed a hand on El Diablo's shoulder. "This is a very long temblor," he said, "but a gentle one. There. Now it has stopped."

Grandfather got up from his chair and hobbled over to the two boys. "Go and get your supper," he told them.

El Diablo walked unsteadily to Grandfather's chair and sat down. He looked pale. Julia brought him a bowl of beans with two tortillas on top. He accepted it solemnly and began to eat. "My God!" he growled to Paco, "these beans *are* hot." He gulped. "Just the way the devil likes them," he said and grinned.

Paco glanced at Amelia. She went serenely about her business, feeding the children and herself.

El Diablo thrust out his bowl. "Give me some more," he ordered. Although it seemed impossible, his manners had grown even worse than they had been at his last visit.

Amelia caught Julia's eye and shook her head slightly. "I'll be glad to serve you, señor," Amelia said, and stepped forward to take his bowl. Paco noticed that she stood well back and snatched the bowl from El Diablo at arm's length before she turned around and carried it back to the bean pot.

Don Porfirio stood near. He took the bowl from Amelia, filled it and put one tortilla on top. "It will be my pleasure to serve your guest," he said with dignity.

El Diablo laughed loudly. "You're the brujo," he observed as he took the bowl with one huge hand. "Did you put something evil into my beans?"

Don Porfirio's eyes flashed. "I put nothing in the beans," he said, "but I can easily put a spell on you and you will then feel great pain. So behave yourself."

"Absurdo," growled El Diablo, but Paco noticed that the hand holding the tortilla trembled for just an instant.

El Diablo finished the beans and handed the empty bowl to Don Porfirio. "I'll be going now," he announced. "Be sure to plant the seeds four inches apart, Paquito. I'll check with you later to make sure you did it right."

The two little boys ran to the gate and peered down the street after him. "He's gone," said Juan.

Grandfather collapsed onto his chair and the children began talking among themselves excitedly. Paco and Amelia exchanged glances. They were keyed up, but careful not to give anything away.

The children stopped talking and looked expectantly at their father. Juan said, "Well, did it work, Papá?"

Paco froze. "What do you mean, Juanito?"

"You know—did he eat the castor beans?"

Paco looked at Amelia in horror. She lifted her eyebrows and shrugged. "Yes," said Paco, "he ate the castor beans. Now how did you learn about this, mi hijo?"

"We heard it at school, Papá. Everyone knows. How long will it take him to die?"

Paco turned to the brujo. "Perhaps you can answer that question, Don Porfirio."

"It's hard to say, Paco, because I don't know exactly how many castor beans the man has eaten. You are not the first to give them to him, you know."

"I didn't know, Don Porfirio, but I'm glad to hear that we're not the only ones. Will it take him a longer time to die because of his great size?"

"I think so, Paco. In fact he may not even get sick for several days."

Don Porfirio took a step toward the children. He glowered at each of them from under his bushy eyebrows, the power in his eyes transfixing them with fear. "You are not to speak of this to anyone," he said fiercely. "Not ever. Do I make myself clear?"

The children edged closer together, their faces solemn, their eyes huge. "Sí, Don Porfirio, it is clear," they said.

Paco felt relieved. He now knew for certain that not one word of this event would ever be told, for the children dreaded the magical powers of the brujo.

So did he, for that matter!

CHAPTER 17

It was early morning. Milly had just awakened when she heard a knock on her door. "Pase," she called.

The door opened and Elpidio blurted, "Patrona, something has happened," then added quickly, as if apologizing for his poor manners, "I mean buenos días, patrona."

"Buenos días, Elpidio. Please sit down and calm yourself." She patted the side of the bed. The bed jiggled. Elpidio had obeyed her, but she noticed that he was sitting on the foot of the bed, as far away from her as he could possibly get. Although he was totally distraught and she was old enough to be his grandmother, by golly Elpidio was ever conscious of the proprieties.

"Now tell me what's troubling you," she said.

"It's about the trap, patrona."

"Aha—did we catch the cat this time?"

"No, patrona, we did not catch the cat. What's more, the trap is broken and there is a huge footprint beside it."

"You mean like a jaguar footprint?"

"No, patrona, it is a human footprint, the biggest I have ever seen!"

El Diablo!

Milly felt her heart fly against her ribs and flutter there

before it settled back to a steady but livelier beat. She told herself that Elpidio was mistaken, that El Diablo could not get inside the walls of Casa Colonial at night. Margarita always put the chain on the front door before she went to bed. No, it was impossible.

"Could there be two footprints together, Elpidio, making it look like one huge print?"

Elpidio seemed offended that she would question his judgment in this important matter. "Absolutely not, patrona. I can tell one footprint when I see it, and this is one footprint. Unquestionably." He lowered his voice to a conspiratorial murmur. "I believe that the cat is a náhual, an evil spirit. It must have gone into the trap to eat the bait, and then it could not get out. In order to escape, it had to turn itself into a giant, thus breaking the trap. The dog knows, patrona, and that is why it barks every night. We must find a brujo at once to get rid of this náhual."

"Let me think about it," Milly said. "Please leave the trap and everything around it just as it is—and say nothing to anyone. When Inocencio gets here, we'll ask his advice. Don't worry, Elpidio, we'll all work together on this problem."

"What shall I say to Leslie, Patrona?"

"Say nothing at all unless he asks you. If he asks, tell him that you don't have time to talk and you'll see him after breakfast. Can you do that?"

"Sí, patrona. Of course I can do that, but—"

"Then just take care of your duties in the garden, Elpidio. When Inocencio comes, he and I will look at the damage and decide what to do. Meanwhile, I'll get dressed right away."

Milly took a quick shower that was not much more than a splash, and threw on some clothes. She understood that Elpidio was agitated about having a náhual in the trap because he believed in such things wholeheartedly. But to her, the footprint spoke of El Diablo and danger to her household. Elpidio might have exaggerated the size of the footprint to enhance his story, but she couldn't be sure about that. And how *did* the trap get broken? If only she could take a look at it for herself. She clenched her fists and shook her head, hating her helplessness.

Now, now; none of that! Herbert's voice scolded somewhere inside her mind.

Milly reacted with such resentment that she surprised herself. "I'll damned well get upset if I want to!" she said loudly. "I'm the one who has to deal with this mess, not you." She heaved a sigh of disgust. "Oh, I suppose you're right, Herbie. Elpidio is probably all stirred up over nothing and we'll sort it out easily once Inocencio gets here."

In spite of her brave words, Milly could not face the thought of going to the dining room and making small talk at breakfast. Instead, she walked over to the office and dropped into the leather chair beside Inocencio's desk to wait for him. After a few impatient minutes she phoned his house, fumbling to place her fingers in the correct holes of the telephone dial. Lidia told her that Inocencio had already left for work and should be there any minute. Finally, Milly went into the sala, sat on the sofa and pulled her braille book from under the cushion. She opened it at random and placed her fingertips on the page. At that very moment she heard Inocencio's key in the lock.

"Well it's about time," she muttered. She slammed her book, stuffed it back under the cushion, and trotted down the length of the sala and out the door as fast as she could go.

"Inocencio!" she called. "Oh, I'm so glad you're here. Please come with me to the vacant lot."

Inocencio laughed. "What happened, did you catch a *tigre?*"

"This is not a joke, señor. I need you to be my eyes."

"Very well, señora, we'll look at your cat trap as soon as I make a couple of phone calls. Just give me a few minutes here."

"No! This is important and we need to do it now!"

Milly knew that Inocencio's back went up whenever she issued orders. She softened her tone, hoping to persuade him with a minimum of stress. "Please," she said, "I need you to inspect the trap and the ground around it very carefully. I won't tell you what I think is there. I'll wait for you to tell me exactly what you see."

"Come on, then," he grumbled, and led the way at such a lively clip that Milly was hard pressed to keep up.

Inocencio liked to do things his own way at his own pace. She knew that. All she could do at the moment was ignore his ill humor as they trotted down the orchid arbor, turned left onto the veranda, right around the far end of the house and into the empty lot.

"My, my, I see a path," Inocencio said sarcastically. "Elpidio must come here very often."

Milly followed silently, so close on his heels now that when he stopped, she ran into him. "Sorry," she mumbled and stepped back to wait for his observations.

"Ay-yi," said Inocencio, "the trap has been smashed almost flat. I wonder how that happened."

"Do you see anything on the ground around it?"

"The bait is scattered and is drawing insects. Oh-oh! There's a footprint. No wonder you said this was important. I'd say that El Diablo has been here."

"Are you sure?"

"A footprint this big could not have been made by anyone else. I wonder how he got in. Did he come to the house last evening to visit Rodolfo Sánchez?"

"Not that I know of, unless one of the muchachas let him in without telling me."

"I'll find out if any of them have seen him. Meanwhile, remember that you have a bus and a guide coming this morning. They should be here in about half an hour."

"Omigod," groaned Milly, "we're going to the wood carvers today. I'd forgotten all about it."

"Well, you promised to take the guests, so you'll have to do it. While you're at San Martín I'll look into this business of El Diablo and the broken trap."

"I really hate to leave while all this is going on, but you're right, I have to go. Come to think of it, I haven't even had breakfast yet. Before you got here, I was too nervous to eat."

"You'd better put something in your stomach, señora. There's a long morning ahead for both of us."

"When I get back from San Martín, I hope you'll be able to tell me exactly what happened here, Inocencio. By the way, I'm sure that Sánchez won't go with us, so ask him any questions you need to—and don't bother about being polite!"

Milly hurried to the dining room. Everyone else had finished breakfast and the room was empty. She didn't feel a bit hungry, but forced herself to eat a slice of fresh pineapple. After that, oatmeal, scrambled eggs, toast and strawberry jam went down quite easily. As she gulped a second cup of coffee Herbert's voice popped into her head. *Mildred*, he said with a laugh, *the day that you can't eat will probably be the day you die.*

Well, she quipped silently, *I guess I'm safe for the moment.*

She trotted off to her cottage, grabbed her purse and headed out to the front door. She was the last one onto the bus. Her usual seat just behind the driver was empty and waiting.

Yolanda moved from the back and slid in beside her. The two of them had seemed to share a certain comradeship since the head-patting incident.

As the bus pulled away from the curb, Milly thought about the broken trap, and suddenly it struck her like a roundhouse punch that last night as the house slept, El Diablo, a supposed murderer, had been roaming the grounds of Casa Colonial freely. He could have peered into bedrooms, watching people. He might even have entered the cottage and stood over her while she slept. It was a terrifying thought. If she'd pictured it in just that way while she was at the breakfast table she wouldn't have been able to eat a bite!

"You seem worried this morning, Milly," said Yolanda. "Are you feeling okay?"

"I'm just fine." Milly forced a smile and searched her mind for an explanation that might be acceptable. "I guess I was thinking about the streets of San Martín. They're badly rutted from the wooden wheels of oxcarts, and it's pretty rough going as you walk from house to house."

"I'll help you. Don't worry."

Don't worry. Right.

Herbert scolded gently: *Mildred, if you can't do anything about it, just bless it and give it to God.*

I'll do my best, Milly replied meekly.

San Martín Tilcajete was as charming as Milly remembered. She told herself to relax and enjoy the outing as much as she could. The group left the bus and made its way along a shaded dirt track, going first to the house of Epifanio Fuentes. Yolanda took Milly's arm in a comforting grip and Milly smiled at her. There was a high adobe wall in front of Casa Fuentes. The guide pounded on the wooden door and they entered a patio that was large and partly shaded.

"Epifanio is famous for carving angels," Milly said. "His wife paints them, and they're really lovely. I wouldn't mind having a guardian angel, myself," she added wistfully as she thought of El Diablo.

Leslie came running over to her. "I found the most fantastic carving," he said. "It's a boy angel with brown hair and tall, silver wings. He's been painted in a plaid, button-down shirt, jeans and running shoes."

Milly laughed. "He sounds just like you, Leslie—except that you're no angel. You should get it."

"Can't," he replied. "It costs a hundred dollars."

Yolanda spoke up eagerly. "Show me where it is. If you're not going to buy it, maybe I will. Do you mind?"

Leslie produced a dramatic shrug. "I guess not. Sure— go ahead."

Down the street and around the corner was the home

and shop of Jesús Sosa. Milly found a wooden frog there that felt lovely and smooth to the touch. Yolanda told her that it was painted all over with irregular lavender spots outlined in red and black. Milly said, "I'll bet they're amoebas. Jesús told me one time that he went to the doctor and saw a book with pictures in it of the organisms that cause amoebic dysentery. He thought they were so interesting that he's been painting them on his carvings ever since, and in all sorts of different colors."

Later, when they arrived at the Margarito Melchor household, Milly called Leslie over. She felt sorry for him because Yolanda had bought his angel.

"This family specializes in cats," she told him. "In view of all the problems we've had with the trap, don't you think you and I should get a cat?"

"Yeah—great idea!"

"All right, you choose one and I'll pay for it. See if you can find one that's small to medium; Margarito charges by the inch."

Leslie stepped up to the display table. He spent a long time handling the various carvings before he could make up his mind. At last he said, "I want this one, Milly."

"Why this one?"

"Because its face looks kind of happy and surprised, as if somebody just told it a funny story."

He placed the carving in Milly's hands and she measured its length with her fingers. Not too expensive. "Is it red?" she asked.

Leslie rearranged the cat on her palm. "It's lying down with its head turned to one side," he explained. "Yes, the body is painted red with black stripes, and the face is pale blue with eyes and ears the color of apricots."

Milly smiled at the despcription. "It has a wonderful curled up tail," she said as her fingers followed a slim piece of wood up and over the cat's back. "Oh! It has whiskers," she said with delight. "Here's my coin purse. Pay Margarito's wife, and bring back the change, okay?"

As they were walking back to the bus, the guide herded them to one side of the street against a wall. Milly saw movement out in the middle of the street and took a wild guess. "It's a pair of oxen," she said.

"Yes," said Yolanda. "Aren't they big? And so handsome."

The beasts stopped in front of them and a man's voice said, "Buenos días, Doña Milly." He sounded familiar, but she couldn't quite place him.

"Buenos días, señor. Oh! It's Paco. How very nice to see you. What are you doing in San Martín?"

"I'm returning my brother-in-law's oxen, señora. We borrowed them to plant the corn. I hope you are well."

"Gracias, Paco, I am very well. Is everything all right in your household and with your village?"

"Sí, señora, don't worry; the family is happy and the village is peaceful."

Milly knew otherwise, but probing further would only expose Paco's private business to public scrutiny while accomplishing nothing. "Please give my best wishes to Amelia and to everyone at home," she said.

"Sí," chimed in Leslie, "and my best to Julia and her brothers."

"*Igualmente*, señora, the very best to you and the young man from my entire family."

Paco clucked to the oxen, they swung their heads, settled into the yoke, and plodded on down the street.

"Who was that?" asked Yolanda.

"A friend from Santo Tomás Jalieza, the weaving village we went to the other day. I'm very fond of Paco and his family. They're fine people."

"So he's planting corn. That's very interesting. Do they grow anything else at that village?"

"No, mostly just corn and castor beans, plus some maguey and a few vegetables for their own use."

Milly was tempted to tell Yolanda about the crisis the villagers were facing, and the terrible trouble Paco could get into if he were forced to plant marijuana. Don't bother, she told herself. Yolanda can't do anything about it. She has no more influence over her father and El Diablo than I do. Anyway, Leslie was listening.

Everyone climbed onto the bus. The driver started the motor with a roar and they jounced down the road toward the highway.

Yolanda unwrapped the package she held on her lap. "This is the most wonderful angel I've ever seen," she said. "I have the perfect place to put it when I get home."

"I must warn you," said Milly, "that copal wood is full of powder-post beetle eggs. They can hatch and completely demolish your angel from the inside out, without your knowing it. The moment you get it home you must put it in the freezer for at least two weeks. It's the only way I know of to kill those eggs."

Milly was tired of shouting over the roar and rattle of the bus. Besides, seeing Paco had reminded her of the awful problems brewing back at The Casa. She bowed her head and pretended to doze.

By the time the bus stopped in front of the house, she was quite thankful to be home, and more than ready for a cool drink and a rest before dinner.

Yolanda was the first person off the bus, and turned back to help Milly. As they moved together across the sidewalk, Milly placed her left hand on Yolanda's arm and smiled at her. Yolanda gasped and jerked to a stop as if she'd run into a glass wall.

"What is it?" asked Milly. "What's the matter?"

Yolanda shook free of Milly's hand and ran a few steps down the sidewalk.

"Papá!" she wailed.

Milly turned her head back and forth, straining to see what fragments she could against the glare of sunlight. She spotted what might be a bundle of clothes lying in front of Yolanda in the angle formed by the house and the sidewalk. Then her vision was cut off completely by people climbing off the bus and swirling around her, talking in excited voices. The bus driver honked the horn repeatedly. Someone ran to the front door, pounding on it and shouting for Inocencio. Somewhere in all the confusion Adriana screamed and screamed.

The door to The Casa banged open and Inocencio ran out. Milly grabbed his arm. "Tell me what's going on," she pleaded. He tried to pull away, but she clung to him. "Dammit!" she shouted in his ear, "*tell me what's happening!*"

Inocencio's voice shook. "It's Rodolfo Sánchez. He's lying on the sidewalk and there's blood all over the place. Now let go of me. I have to call an ambulance."

CHAPTER 18

Milly pushed her way through the crowd gathered around Rodolfo Sánchez. She found Yolanda and Adriana on their knees on the pavement beside him, both sobbing wildly.

"There, there," Milly murmured, and bent forward to put an arm around each of them. "Come, come now," she coaxed, but the two women refused to be comforted; their cries of anguish only swelled. She recalled that Adriana had responded well to high-handed orders at the dinner table during the crisis over Olga's Yalálag cross. Perhaps that approach would work again.

"Stop that crying, Adriana," she commanded, "and do something useful for your husband."

Adriana gulped and her sobs quieted enough for her to say, "What *can* I do for him, Doña Milly? He's dying!"

"Maybe he won't die if you help him. Do you know what happened? Was he mugged?"

"Look! Blood is pouring out of his chest! *Please* help me. We must take him into the house. He needs a doctor right away!"

Yolanda snuffled and hiccupped. "Hush, Mamá," she said. "Inocencio is phoning for an ambulance. It should be here any minute. Papá will be much better off in a hospital."

Adriana persisted. "We cannot leave him here!"

Milly groped in the bottom of her handbag. "Here's a clean handkerchief," she told Yolanda. "Fold it, put it over your father's wound and press hard to stop the bleeding. If we try to move him, we might do him great damage. He should lie here quietly until the ambulance comes."

She raised her voice a little and leaned closer to Sánchez. She ignored the sickening, metallic smell of blood and spoke directly to him. "Can you hear me, Rodolfo?"

He answered in a rasping whisper. "Sí."

"What happened?"

"...came out door...shot."

"Shot? My God!" Now Milly understood! But how could Sánchez have been shot almost on her doorstep without anyone noticing? She leaned closer still and asked, "Who did this, Rodolfo?"

"...nazi..."

Milly drew back, baffled. "You mean a German Nazi?"

Sánchez shook his head and groaned. Milly could tell that he must be in great pain.

"I'm so sorry, my friend. The ambulance is on its way and I promise that we'll take good care of you." She called over her shoulder, "Leslie, will you please ask the driver to move his bus away from the house? We need to make room for the ambulance."

Moments later, the bus not only moved, but took off down the street. Inocencio must have paid the driver and sent him on his way. Milly heard the sound of a police klaxon grow louder and louder as a car skidded around the corner and squealed to a stop in the space just vacated by the bus. The blare of the pulsating klaxon, out of sync with the flashing light on the car's roof, made her dizzy. Added to that was the disgusting odor of blood on the hot pavement. For an instant Milly's stomach lurched and she felt her head spin. She closed her eyes.

After what seemed like ages, but was probably only a

moment, the motor was turned off, and the deafening sound died away. A man jumped out and shoved his way through the crowd.

"*Policía! Policía!*" he shouted. "*Qué pasó?*" What happened here?

Milly's nausea subsided and she turned to face this strident officer of the law. "Señor, there has been a shooting and we are awaiting the ambulance. The victim is unconscious. I suggest that you follow the ambulance to the hospital and interview him there."

The policeman brushed her aside as if she were a pesky mosquito and turned to glower at the group. "*Su atención!*" he yelled in rapid-fire Spanish. "Which one of you stupid *norte americanos* shot this important Mexican citizen?" He waited in vain for an answer, perhaps not realizing that the norte americanos couldn't understand a word he said.

Yolanda addressed him in haughty Spanish. "You are mistaken, señor. This is my father and he was already hurt when we arrived."

Milly felt Leslie's small hand clutch hers. She squeezed it and whispered, "Inocencio must still be on the phone. Bring him out here. Quick!"

To the policeman she said, "No one here shot anybody, señor, for we are all friends. No one even has a gun. We were returning to Casa Colonial from a bus trip and found him like this."

"A bus trip, old woman? I see no bus here," sneered the policeman. "Stop lying to me. I am not a fool, you know!"

Yes, you are! thought Milly, but she was getting panicky. This swaggering idiot had every legal right to throw them all into jail, and since Mexico's penal system was based on the Napoleonic Code, they could all rot there till they proved their innocence.

At that moment Inocencio came out the door, took the policeman aside and spoke to him calmly. Milly heard only snatches of the conversation, but she could tell that Inocencio was eloquent and respectful.

At last the ambulance came skidding around the corner. To her horror, Milly found herself reliving the pain of Herbert's final illness. She remembered that the ambulance had been a pickup truck with an open camper shell and a canvas cot inside; hardly state of the art. But it had served for Herbert, and she hoped it would prove adequate for today's problem. The policeman ran to move his car, the ambulance took its place, and Rodolfo Sánchez was loaded into the back on a stretcher.

Milly said, "Yolanda, you and your mother ride with him in the ambulance. Inocencio and I will come along as soon as we can. Meanwhile, if you need us for anything, just call. The number is in the phone book."

Yolanda helped her mother into the back of the truck and climbed in after her. The ambulance started for the hospital and, to Milly's great relief, the police car followed.

Still shaking from all the excitement, she led the guests through the front door and into the cool dimness of Inocencio's office.

"Sat vas awful!" said Poul. "I hope Rodolfo vill be all right."

"We all hope so," said Milly. "After dinner Inocencio and I will go to the hospital and we'll keep you posted on his condition."

"Are we safe?" George wanted to know. "Has there ever been a shooting around here before?"

"Never! Somewhere out there Rodolfo Sánchez must have an enemy who is extremely violent. That's probably why he never went outside our walls until today. But don't worry, we'll leave everything to the police. They'll find out why he was shot." Judging by the man who'd just been here, Milly didn't think the police were smart enough to find their own elbows on a sunny day, but she wasn't about to say so.

She was just starting for her room when Inocencio said quietly, "Can you wait a little moment, señora? We need to talk."

It was several moments, however, before he was free. In a bizarre reaction to their shock, the vacationers seemed determined to spend their time pleasantly, even in the face of the tragedy they had just witnessed. Milly fretted while Inocencio changed a quantity of dollars into pesos for Elmer. Olga claimed her laundry and attempted to re-negotiate the price. Evelyn and Billie Jo stopped to chat about what had happened.

"That was frightening," Billie Jo said to Milly.

"Yes, I was terrified too! But it's all over now and I'm sure there's no more danger."

"If there's anything we can do to help, be sure to let us know."

"I'll do that, Billie Jo. Thank you very much."

"And now," said Evelyn, "let me pay you for the beautiful wooden cat you got for Leslie."

"Absolutely not!" said Milly, wishing the two women would break up the party and leave. "That was an arrangement between Leslie and me. And I hope the cat will remind him of pleasant times in Oaxaca; not the shooting." Milly wondered, not for the first time, if her attitude toward Leslie were changing just a bit. She kept trying to like him, and today, at least, he had behaved reliably.

When all the guests had gone to their rooms and Elpidio had been dispatched with a scrub brush and a bucket of water to remove the stains on the front sidewalk, Milly said to Inocencio, "Thank you for getting rid of that awful policeman. What on earth did you say to him?"

"I told him the name of the bus company and the name of the driver. I also explained that you are a sterling character who has owned this hotel for many years."

He groaned in sudden anguish, and Milly peered at him with sharp concern.

"And then señora, I gave him two hundred pesos! I hope that was all right."

"All right? It was perfect! The money was probably

what persuaded him to leave."

"I think so. But it also didn't hurt that he is married to Lidia's father's second cousin."

This was so typical of Oaxaca, Milly thought. She couldn't help one nervous little titter as she imagined how severely it must have pained Inocencio to part with that much money, even though it was hers.

She sobered immediately as she thought of Sánchez lying on the sidewalk like a discarded bundle of bloody laundry. "I mustn't laugh," she said guiltily. "This really isn't a laughing matter, not any of it!"

"No," Inocencio said reprovingly, "it isn't. Who do you suppose shot him?"

"I asked him that and he said, 'nazi.'"

"Nazi? What does that mean? Maybe he was out of his head. If you're right about how he earns his living, then he was probably shot by someone in the drug business."

"Yes! And my vote goes to El Diablo, but I wonder if we'll ever know."

Inocencio moved some things from the top of his desk into the drawers. "Just give me a second here to lock up my desk, and then we'll go back to the empty lot. This time *I* have something to show *you*."

It was clear that Inocencio wouldn't talk until they were on the back side of the house and away from other eyes and ears. They retraced the route they had taken earlier this morning, but this time they walked right past the broken trap and up a short rise to the wall at the end of the lot.

Inocencio said, "This is what I want to show you; this old door."

Milly reached out and put both hands on it. It was heavy wood, rough and weathered. Although she had known about this door, and that it was on her property, she had never been to this particular spot before. The door was tucked away among rioting bugambilla vines and tall weeds, and until now there had been no reason for her to come here. Whenever she went to an unfamiliar place she always counted steps and mapped the area in her mind, but today she had been so preoccupied with the shooting that she had forgotten to count. And the path had curved a couple of times, which was disorienting. Serves me right for following Inocencio blindly, she told herself with dark humor.

"Inocencio, I'm afraid you'll have to tell me where we are. Does this door open onto the street?"

"Yes, it does. We walked up the back side of the house past the bedroooms, the dining room and the kitchen, and past the back of room five to this outside wall. If we stepped through this door, we'd be on División Oriente, the street that runs along the side of the house. This door is completely out of sight unless you're looking for it."

"Then this must be the old door you told Rodolfo Sánchez wouldn't open because the lock and hinges are rusted. Is that right?"

"That is exactly right, señora! Now watch." Inocencio took something out of his pocket.

"What's that?"

"It's a key."

Milly heard the soft rasp of metal against metal, a gentle click, and the door moved smoothly under her hands, swinging toward her without making a sound.

"Dear sweet Jesus!" she breathed. "What has been going on here?"

"A long time ago I found this big, iron key in the bottom drawer of the desk. I felt sure it was for this door, but it wouldn't work then because the lock was completely rusted. Today it works perfectly."

"You're telling me that someone has repaired and oiled this lock and the hinges?"

"Yes. And it wouldn't be hard to make a duplicate key; the lock is old and very simple. Judging by the giant footprint next to the trap, I'd say that El Diablo comes and goes through this door whenever he feels like it, and other people may be doing the same thing. Señora, it's possible that Rodolfo Sánchez has been operating a drug business right out of Casa Colonial."

CHAPTER 19

"God!" said Milly. "No wonder the dog barks every night!"

"Yes," agreed Inocencio. "He did his best to tell you that strangers were coming through this door, but you wouldn't listen."

"Oh, I listened—every night I listened!—but I was too dumb to get the message. Inocencio, I want you to block off this door right away. El Diablo is a killer and we've got to keep him out of here!"

Inocencio hesitated for a long moment. "We could fasten this door shut with no trouble at all, but it seems to me that the problem is not that simple. If it becomes known that there is drug trafficking out of Casa Colonial, the government could confiscate your business and throw you out of the country. I think it would be better to leave the door just as it is. Then later, when we have proof of what's going on, we can call in the police."

"Why not just nail it shut and call them now?"

"Because El Diablo has undoubtedly given bribes to the police department. I'm afraid *we'll* be arrested—you and me!—if we accuse Sánchez and El Diablo without providing good evidence that they're criminals."

"Oh, dear, what a mess! How can we possibly get proof of that?"

"Now that is an interesting problem, señora. It is my opinion that we'll have to let El Diablo come through this door while we watch what he does. That is the only way I can think of to get proof."

"What—and have him creeping through the garden again tonight? That's easy for *you* to say. *You* go home before supper, but I have to stay here! How can I sleep knowing that bad people are walking around in the dark outside my room?"

"Well—lock your door."

"That sounds very flimsy. I guess I can sit up in my rocking chair with Herbert's old pistol in my lap." Milly shuddered. "I don't want to shoot anybody. What if I plug Margarita by mistake—or blow away my own foot! Anyway, we have to consider the guests. If I'm in danger, they are too. It's our responsibility to protect them."

The dinner bell rang faintly on the other side of the house. Milly turned to leave, but Inocencio didn't budge and she couldn't find her way without him. She clenched her fists in frustration. Her very worst blind spot was when she looked down at the ground in front of her. She was never able to see where to place her feet. She waited impatiently while Inocencio shut the door and re-locked it.

At last he started down the path and she fell in behind him, watching the dim outline of his small body bob along ahead of her. She lifted her feet high and stepped carefully, determined not to stumble.

Over his shoulder Inocencio said, "You're right, señora, it is our duty to protect everyone in the house. Let's talk about it again after siesta. Between us we'll come up with something. Don't worry."

"Everybody keeps telling me not to worry," Milly said angrily. "Of course I'll worry! How can I help it?"

Somehow she managed to get through dinner. Her Gracious-Hostess persona performed almost of its own accord while her Inner-Self churned over the very nasty fact that Casa Colonial, her sanctum, had been violated flagrantly and repeatedly. The sensation of being two separate people at once compounded her distress, and she entertained a fleeting thought that her current mental state might be akin to schizophrenia.

It was no comfort that the talk at the table was all about who had shot Rodolfo Sánchez, and why.

"He vas such a shy, inoffensive man," said Poul, speaking as if Sánchez were already dead. "I can't imagine somevun vanting to kill him."

Milly smothered a derisive snort. She could almost imagine polishing off rotten old Sánchez herself.

Elmer said, "Rudy wasn't all *that* wonderful. At times he could be a real asshole."

"Watch your language, Elmer!" ordered Billie Jo.

"I had only one conversation with him," observed Evelyn, "but he seemed to adore his wife and daughter and was always looking for ways to please them."

"He liked to buy them things," said George, "but he wouldn't leave the house to go shopping. A strange and interesting man."

"Goin' outside the house today sure turned out to be one helluva mistake," said Elmer. "Too bad he picked today for a change of scenery."

Bad luck indeed, thought Milly. "Does anyone know what he did for a living?" she asked.

"He knew a lot about the New York Stock Exchange," said Elmer, "but as far as I know, he was retired. I don't know what from. Import-export, maybe."

Import-export, eh? Like import dollars, export marijuana! With a superhuman effort Milly refrained from sharing that theory. She longed to lay out all her information and get feedback from the people around her, but quite simply it was not good business to frighten the guests. People waited all year and saved their money to buy a pleasant vacation, and it should *be* pleasant.

For the same reason, she buttoned her lip about El Diablo. Inocencio had told her that they'd figure out a way to foil the man, and that was good enough for her. She had every confidence in Inocencio.

The moment dinner was over, she went looking for him.

"I want to go to the hospital to see if I can help Adriana and Yolanda," she told him. "Can you go with me?"

"Yes, I can go right now. Let me call Roberto to bring his taxi."

"I'll get my hat and purse and be back in a minute," Milly said. As she headed down the path toward her cottage, Leslie came running up and slipped his sticky little hand into hers. His fingers twitched and he seemed...well, fearful. This was such a change from the usual brash Leslie that Milly stopped and turned to face him. She grasped his hand in both of hers, trying to communicate a feeling of calm to the child. "Is something the matter?" she asked.

"I went to look at the trap just now," he said in a frightened voice. "It's busted all to hell and I saw a giant footprint in the dust. That big dude who chased us in the market must want to get even with me for tying his shoelaces to the counter. How does he know where I'm staying?"

Milly didn't know what to say. She didn't believe in lying to a child, but it was clear that Leslie needed reassurance. What truth could she tell without frightening him even more? "I think you're right about who it is," she said slowly. "I have no idea why he broke the trap, but I don't think he did it because of you, Leslie."

"Why else would he come here?"

"Because he has another connection at this house; one that has nothing to do with you. The first time he came to Casa Colonial, you hadn't even arrived in Oaxaca yet." She stopped, careful not to give away too much information.

"Who is this other connection?"

"I'd better not say, Leslie. I don't want to get you involved in this."

Leslie's hand moved convulsively in hers. "I'll bet it was Señor Sánchez! And I'll bet the big guy was the one who shot him!"

"It's a possibility," Milly admitted. "Now listen, Leslie, you and I can speculate about this to each other, but we shouldn't mention it to anyone else."

"Why not?"

"Because we're just guessing. If word of our suspicions should get back to that big man, it would make him very angry and even more dangerous. We have no evidence, you see."

"Then I'll just have to *find* some evidence." Leslie had snapped back to his old self. He jerked his hand out of Milly's and ran off before she could stop him.

"Don't do anything," she yelled after him. "Leave it to the grownups."

Herbert's voice murmured in her mind, *Save your breath. There's no way anyone can set the brakes on that kid.*

By the time Milly met Inocencio at the front door, Roberto had just pulled up in his taxi. They climbed in and she leaned her head against the back of the seat and closed her eyes. Things were getting just too darned chaotic. She felt worn to a frazzle.

Roberto guided the taxi away from the curb and moved it expertly through the traffic.

Inocencio said, "I think I have found Rodolfo Sánchez' brother Victor."

"No kidding! Where is he?"

"Well, I should say that I found out where he was. He's not there any more. He checked into the Hotel Villareal about six weeks ago. He spent his time coming and going like any other tourist, and then a week or two ago he disappeared. He left no forwarding address, so they don't know what to do with his things. I told them I'd send

Elpidio to pick them up tomorrow."

"What do you suppose happened to him?"

"I have a very bad feeling about Victor Sánchez. I think he was probably the other corpse that Paco found in his cornfield. By this time I'll bet he's buried somewhere out in the hills. No one will ever find him."

Roberto stopped the taxi and backed it into a parking space.

"Where are we?" asked Milly.

"In front of the Corazón de Jesús Clinic," said Inocencio. "I told the ambulance driver to bring Rodolfo Sánchez here. It's very expensive and has only a dozen rooms, but the doctors are good and the care is excellent."

"Sánchez won't mind the expense," Milly said drily.

As they climbed the front stairs she said, "Let's not say anything about Rodolfo's brother just yet. These people have enough on their minds without hearing bad news about Victor."

Inocencio opened the front door for her and they walked into the lobby. "Oh-oh," he said, "there's that policeman."

"I don't want to answer a bunch of questions," said Milly. "C'mon!" She dodged to her right down a short hallway, moving at her usual brisk trot.

Inocencio grabbed her elbow and steered her around another corner to her left. He found a nurse who could lead them to the room of Rodolfo Sánchez. Adriana and Yolanda jumped up to greet them with tearful abrazos.

The light in the room was dim and Milly couldn't see a thing. "How is he?" she whispered, trying not to disturb the patient.

"He's in surgery right now," said Adriana. "They're removing the bullet and assessing the damage."

"Oh," said Milly in normal tones. "Did he tell you anything more about who did this to him?"

"No, Milly, he hasn't spoken at all."

Someone brought two more chairs, and they sat around

the perimeter of the small room, staring at the empty bed and each other, waiting for news. There didn't seem to be anything to say.

The minutes dragged by. At last, the doctor came in and spoke to Adriana. "The damage is not as bad as I first thought," he told her in a business-like way. "The bullet entered the upper left side of the chest and exited through the back of the shoulder. He lost a lot of blood and one rib was nicked, but the bullet missed the artery and the lung. He's a very lucky man!"

"Oh, thank God!" whispered Yolanda.

"Now then, *when* he can be discharged from the hospital depends on several things besides his physical condition. Señora, tell me, please, exactly who shot him."

"No one knows, Doctor."

"That's too bad. If we could identify the assailant we could protect your husband from another attack. As it is, I guess Señor Sánchez will have to leave the clinic within the next few hours."

"So soon, Doctor? I'm anxious to take him home, of course, but for the sake of his health shouldn't he remain in your care overnight, at least?"

"Ordinarily, señora, a patient with this type of wound would be hospitalized for several days. However, the police have warned us that whoever shot your husband may try again. The chief of police, himself, advised us to discharge your husband immediately and send him back to Mexico City in an ambulance."

"You can't do that," protested Yolanda. "The ambulance is a very rough ride and it's a ten-hour trip. My father would be in pain the whole time and he could easily bleed to death before we got him home."

"Sorry, we've had our orders."

"At least give us time to arrange for a private airplane to come down from Mexico City."

Adriana began to sob. "Don't do this to us," she pleaded.

"Señora, we have no choice. We can't risk anyone shooting at him here in our hospital. Our first duty is to protect the other patients and our staff."

Nonsense, thought Milly. She had listened to all this talk with increasing disbelief. If this were the United States there'd be policemen all over the place and they'd damn well protect both Sánchez and the clinic. She felt her anger rise. "A hospital should feel concern for *all* its patients," she said haughtily, "and Rodolfo Sánchez is your patient. You should place an armed guard outside his door and continue to care for him properly."

"No es posible."

Milly was shocked by the coldness of this dictum. It was practically a death sentence and had been delivered without any apparent feeling.

"Bring him to Casa Colonial," she blurted. "*We're* not cowards. We'll take care of him until he's able to travel."

The moment the words were out of her mouth, Milly knew she'd made a promise that she couldn't keep. For one thing, round-the-clock nurses and armed guards might be impossible to find on short notice, and Sánchez' very presence would draw danger to the household. Anyway, would she really turn the place upside down, putting everyone at risk for this despicable old drug lord? No, she wouldn't; but she might attempt it for his long-suffering wife and daughter.

As she turned the possibility over in her mind, the matter was taken out of her hands. She heard the strident voice of the policeman who had appeared right after Sánchez had been shot, the one she and Inocencio had avoided by sneaking down the hospital corridor. He spoke pompously.

"The State of Oaxaca considers Rodolfo Sánchez to be an undesirable person. He is to leave the hospital by ambulance as soon as it is dark and will be accompanied by a police escort as far as the state border. This order comes straight from the governor's office and will be enforced by the Chief of State Police."

So git outta Dodge! Herbert's voice drawled in her mind.

Milly shook her head in amazement. The authorities are turning on Sánchez, she thought. Their pockets are lined with his bribe money, but with a bullet in him, he's no longer useful to them. Or maybe someone else is paying them more. They're turning on him and he's going to die. Truly, there is no honor among thieves. She opened her mouth to tell this policeman that she didn't like him and that she found his orders intolerable, but she felt Inocencio's warning hand on her arm.

"Be quiet," he murmured in English. "There's nothing you can do, so let it go. Maybe their way is best."

Milly struggled not to burst into tears of sheer frustration. She held a deep and abiding sympathy for Adriana and Yolanda. And in spite of her contempt for Rodolfo Sánchez, she felt it imperative, for his family's sake, to see that he was treated humanely. If she were to live in Oaxaca for a thousand years, she could never learn to accept the cold practicality of the Mexican police.

"You ride in the ambulance with Papá," she heard Yolanda say gently to her mother. "I'll come later."

"No, no, mi hija! You must come with us. What if he dies on the way? I cannot do this alone."

"You won't be alone, Mamá; God will be with you. I know you can handle it. Papá will want you with him. I'll go back to Casa Colonial with Doña Milly and wrap up my affairs there. I'll pack all of our things and grab a flight out of here early tomorrow morning. Don't try to meet me. I'll take a cab home from the Mexico City airport. Be brave, Mamá. I'll see the two of you before noon tomorrow."

Milly's ears pricked to an odd tone in Yolanda's voice. What did she mean, her "affairs?" And how could she not want to ride with her parents? She heard the subdued rumble of a gurney rolling down the hall toward them. It sounded like thunder far away in the high mountains. It sounded like doom.

"Here comes Sánchez," said the policeman. "Get ready. We leave soon after dark."

CHAPTER 20

Yolanda put in an appearance at supper, but she was preoccupied and teary. Everyone offered sympathy, then Milly led the conversation along more cheerful pathways. They all jumped in, even Leslie, making an effort to lift the young woman's spirits; a touching display of kindness.

After supper, Milly walked down the veranda to offer moral support while Yolanda packed for tomorrow's journey. The room was a jumble of open suitcases and packing boxes. Milly had to feel her way carefully as she crossed the room. She pushed aside a pile of shoes on one of the twin beds and sat down beside them. As Yolanda pulled her clothes out of the closet, the wire coathangers scraped across the metal pole, adding to the general chaos and setting Milly's teeth on edge.

"Yolanda, for my own peace of mind I need to ask you a rather painful question. Do you remember that before the ambulance came this morning I asked your father if he knew who shot him?"

"Yes, Doña Milly, I remember all too well."

"The only thing he said was 'nazi.' What does that mean?"

"I'm not sure. I've been turning it over in my mind all afternoon." Yolanda sat down on the other bed. "I thought he might have been trying to say my lover's name, though why he would do that, I can't imagine."

"I'm afraid I've forgotten what your young man's name is," said Milly.

"Ignacio. But we always called him Nacio."

Milly thought this over. She decided that if Rodolfo Sánchez had tried to say "Nacio," but couldn't make it through the last syllable, the word "Nazi" made sense. Almost.

"Right at that instant your father was in a lot of pain. It seems very odd that he would choose that particular moment to mention the name of a man he hated. Is it possible that your father was telling us that Ignacio shot him?"

"Absolutely not! Nacio wouldn't dare...wouldn't think of doing such a thing."

"Perhaps your father was speaking to *you*, trying to tell you that he felt guilty about his quarrel with Ignacio."

"Doña Milly, I have no idea what was going through his mind at that moment."

"Is Ignacio here in Oaxaca?"

"Yes." She paused. "Maybe because Papá had been shot and feared he was dying he felt that he should make his peace with Nacio."

"Why? For your sake?"

"Yes, but not just for me," muttered Yolanda. "After all, they used to be partners and best friends."

Milly's mind skipped along as she searched for a gentle way to tell Yolanda the news about Rodolfo's brother Victor. She said, "I'm afraid I have one more unpleasant thing to discuss with you, Yolanda. Inocencio has discovered that your Uncle Victor was staying at the Hotel Villareal, but he's not there any longer."

"Where did he go?"

"His suitcases and all his things are still at the hotel, but I'm afraid Victor has disappeared."

"Oh, my God! He actually did it!"

"Did what?"

Yolanda stood up and ran out the door, crying.

Milly was now completely bewildered. It sounded vaguely as if Yolanda's Uncle Victor had threatened suicide at one time. Could that be what happened to him? Perhaps El Diablo was not responsible for Victor's disappearance, after all. She wondered if she should follow Yolanda and try to calm her.

Before Milly could get to her feet, the door opened again and Yolanda rushed in with an armload of clothing she evidently had collected in her parents' room. She seemed quite composed.

Milly was amazed at this emotional flip-flop. Yolanda had left the room on a wave of hysterics and returned in mere moments, completely unruffled.

"I'm sorry that I upset you," Milly said drily.

"It's okay."

"I hated being the one to give you such terrible news, but it's something your family has to know." Curious, Milly waited for Yolanda's next response.

She said impatiently, "It's all right, Milly. We all take chances when we're in business." She walked over to the other bed and began to fold the clothes and put them into the suitcase. "It's going to take forever to pack my things and all my parents' clothes too."

Milly took the hint and stood up. "Well, I'll let you get on with it. Elpidio is still here, so if you need any help, don't hesitate to call him."

She groped her way across the room and out the door. As she walked around the veranda, turning on the patio lights, she noticed that it was getting quite dark. Very soon now, poor Adriana and Rodolfo would be forced out of the hospital and into that awful ambulance to head for Mexico City. Milly wondered how they could possibly make it home safely.

Quite unexpectedly she found Inocencio still at his

desk in the office. She said, "It's way past suppertime. Shouldn't you be at home by now? Lidia will be worried."

"I phoned Lidia so she knows I'm here. I promised you I'd do something, so I'm going to stay all night and take care of you."

"You are?"

"Yes. It's dangerous to leave you here all by yourself. And anyway, I want to see who comes through that door in the vacant lot."

Herbert's voice said, *Hooray! Give that little bugger a big hug!* Milly managed to control the impulse and Inocencio's dignity remained intact.

Instead, she said warmly, "It's far too dangerous for you to do this all by yourself, Inocencio. We need to find someone to help you."

"Oh, I won't be alone. Elpidio is staying, too, and I called Ernesto Fuentes, that young policeman from Xochitlán. He'll be on duty in Oaxaca tonight, so we can call him over here in a hurry in case we need to take any official action."

"Good! I trust Ernesto. Now then—it gives me the shivers to think about it, but do you suppose El Diablo is out there somewhere keeping watch on this house?"

"I'm sure he is. At least that's what I'd be doing if I were El Diablo. I'd spy on Sánchez either here or over at the hospital. But señora, that makes me think of something worrisome: El Diablo may not come back here tonight or ever again."

"Why not?"

"If he thinks Sánchez is dead, or still at the hospital, there's no reason for him to show up."

"I'd be terribly grateful if I never saw him again," said Milly, speaking from the heart, "but we do need him to come here."

"You're right, señora. We need to learn why he's been coming here in the middle of the night and what he does while he's here."

"I agree, Inocencio, so I think we'd better give him a *reason* to come."

She squinted, gazing toward the garden as she racked her brain for an idea. "I know!" she said with an excited grin. "Have one of your sons sneak over to the hospital and wait there. We'll send an ambulance to pick him up. The attendants can cover him with a blanket, carry him out of the hospital on a stretcher and load him into the back of the ambulance. They should come straight to Casa Colonial and bring him right through our front door. If El Diablo is snooping around out there in the dark, he'll think it's Rodolfo Sánchez coming home from the hospital. Then later, about one in the morning, El Diablo will surely come through the old door in the empty lot to visit Sánchez, as usual."

"It's confusing, señora. I thought Sánchez was avoiding El Diablo."

"That was probably just a ruse so we wouldn't suspect that they were still running a drug business together." She waited for Inocencio's reaction and was astounded to hear his distinctive, high-pitched giggle.

"You should have been a spy," he said admiringly. "You are very deviant."

"I hope you mean 'devious.' But thank you for the compliment."

"Now that you mention it, señora, perhaps I should have a few more people to back me up here tonight. El Diablo is a huge, violent man. If it's all right with you, I'll ask a couple of my grown-up sons to come over."

"I think that's a very good idea." For one startling moment, Milly pictured El Diablo on his back, being tied down by a swarm of Inocencio's sons. Sort of like Gulliver and the Lilliputians.

Inocencio went to the telephone and made two calls. When he returned to his desk he said with satisfaction, "Lidia's great-nephew on her mother's side owns an ambulance. Half an hour from now he'll drive it over to the hospital, pick up my son Alberto and his wife and bring them to Casa Colonial. Alberto will be on the stretcher and Juana will play the part of Señora Adriana. Later on, three more of my sons and two of my nephews will arrive here. They'll be on foot and will come at different times, very quietly, and I'll be here to let them in."

Milly almost laughed aloud. Good old Inocencio. If the occasion called for it, he could probably raise a squadron of stealth bombers, all expertly piloted by his wife's relatives.

"We'll have plenty of time to set up for these maneuvers," said Milly. "I don't think you can expect El Diablo before one or two in the morning. That's when the dog always barks."

"Whenever he comes, we'll be ready for him."

Milly went into the sala, making a grand effort to seem relaxed and to put her guests at ease. She played several games of solitaire, but she was too excited to concentrate. She didn't even care when Elmer sat down across the table and played the game for her. She just kept turning up cards regularly, three at a time.

By and by her thoughts turned to the strange conversation she'd had with Yolanda a little while ago. At the time, everything Yolanda said had seemed perfectly logical. But now, from a perspective free of emotion and sharpened by tension, Milly sensed that some things about their talk didn't ring true. She remembered Yolanda saying, "Oh, my God! He actually did it!" Who actually did what? Milly had wanted to know. But Yolanda had escaped to the room next door, perhaps to avoid having to explain.

And then there was the surprising announcement that Ignacio had been her father's partner and best friend before the big blowup. "Best friend" Milly had already heard about, but "partner?" How many partners did Rodolfo Sánchez have, anyway? They seemed to be proliferating at a great rate. First there'd been El Diablo, the ex-partner. Then she'd learned about Victor Sánchez, the brother and original partner. And now she was hearing about Ignacio, yet another ex-partner. Victor and Rodolfo seemed to be the two constants in this ever-expanding equation, only now Victor was probably dead and Rodolfo had one foot in the grave and the other on a banana peel, as Herbert would say. Something was haywire, but she couldn't quite put her finger on it yet.

Elmer's voice cut into her thoughts. "We've lost the game, here, Milly. Better shuffle and lay 'em out again."

Yes, thought Milly, that's exactly what I need to do!

Absentmindedly, she let her fingers shuffle the cards while her brain reorganized what facts she knew about the Sánchez family and inserted some items of speculation here and there.

Apparently, Rodolfo and Victor had been the founding fathers of the company, so to speak. Then they had taken in two younger partners, El Diablo and Ignacio. Was this younger pair trying to eliminate the brothers in order to take over the business? That didn't feel quite right to Milly, mostly because Rodolfo had told her that he was retired. If that were true, he shouldn't be a threat, so why try to kill him? On the other hand, maybe Rodolfo had lied to her. She wouldn't put it past him.

Yolanda had said that in spite of being under her mother's thumb, she was still seeing Ignacio almost every day. How could she do that, Milly wondered, unless she sneaked out at night—or unless *he* found a way to come to *her*! Aha. Perhaps Ignacio was the one who had upset the dog every night by coming through the old door. He could have sneaked into the vacant lot, gone down the path, through the garden and crept into room seven to visit his Yolanda. Yes, that made sense. The puzzling part was that the footprint beside the broken trap had almost certainly been made by El Diablo. The conclusion seemed inescapable: all this time, both of the younger partners had been invading her premises every night. Wild terrors flew into her head. My God, she thought, we're being overrun by Mexico City gangsters!

As she laid out the cards, she pummelled her thoughts into a semi-logical pattern and discovered that two pieces of the puzzle were still missing. The first was motive for the shooting. The second, a seemingly minor detail, was El Diablo's real name. Out of thin air, almost, she plucked the only name in this sordid affair that she couldn't put together with a face. What if, she mused, El Diablo's real name were Ignacio? Abruptly, the missing pieces snapped into place. How could she have been so stupid? On the other hand, how could anyone have possibly guessed?

"Of course!" she said disgustedly. "They're the same person!"

"What did you say?" asked Elmer.

"Never mind," she replied and handed him the cards. "Here," she urged, "finish the game without me. I have to find Inocencio."

Milly hustled out onto the veranda, took nine rapid steps to her left, turned left again and stood holding onto the chair beside Inocencio's desk. She thought to herself, No wonder Yolanda is always late for breakfast; she's been in her room whooping it up with El Diablo every night. And no wonder she's so emotional; she's probably suffering from sleep deprivation.

There was a loud knock and Inocencio jumped to open the door. In came two men carrying a stretcher. Right behind them walked a woman crying softly. It was a very convincing performance. At least Milly was impressed.

And then it came over her in a flash that all this play-acting was unnecessary. They didn't have to lure El Diablo onto the premises. He'd come anyway, not to visit Rodolfo Sánchez, but as Yolanda's lover, Ignacio. In fact, it was a safe bet that nothing could keep him away.

"Put Don Rodolfo in Room Eight," Inocencio said loudly. "Here, I'll show you the way. Where's Margarita? We need her help." He closed the front door.

Immediately the man on the stretcher tossed off the blanket and rolled to his feet. "Buenas noches, Doña

Milly," he said, his voice taut with excitement.

"Buenas noches, Alberto y Juana. Thank you both for coming."

"*Qué pasa?*" What's going on?

"Your father will tell you all about it. He's the boss tonight."

"Come with me," said Inocencio. "I'll show you what I want you to do. Thanks for helping," he told the driver. "Wait five minutes and then you can pack up the stretcher and leave. Okay?"

Inocencio was gone before Milly could deliver her momentous news. She dropped into the chair beside his desk, determined not to budge until he returned. He *must* hear what she had to say, even if she had to kick him in the shins to get his attention.

After a bit, the ambulance driver left and Juana went with him. A few minutes later Inocencio seemed to materialize from out of the dark patio and sit down at his desk.

Milly leaned forward. "I have something astounding to tell you..." she began.

The doorbell rang and Inocencio jumped to his feet. Milly heard the lock click and the door swing open. Very quietly Inocencio said, "Come in, Tonio," and another son stepped over the threshold. "Let's go through the garden," he said, "and on the way, I'll explain what I want you to do."

"Just a minute!" said Milly. "There's something important I want to say before you disappear again."

"I'm awfully busy. Can't it wait?"

"No, it can't. You need to know this, so listen to me. Yolanda has a boyfriend named Ignacio. He's been coming through the old door and visiting her every night."

"Really?" he answered with gentle sarcasm. "It's a wonder he and El Diablo haven't run into each other. I guess they both have keys, eh?"

Milly had no trouble getting the point: Inocencio was busy deploying his troops and had no time for some flighty female's report on a romance. She held her ground, speaking with exaggerated patience and clarity. "They need only one key because El Diablo's real name is Ignacio."

"So they're both named Ignacio. Quite a coincidence."

Milly grabbed the front of his shirt with both hands and shook him. "Listen to me," she pleaded. "I thought there were two men, but I was wrong. There is only one and he is Yolanda's lover. Forget El Diablo; he and Ignacio are the same person. Furthermore, I don't see how Yolanda can be so deeply involved with him without knowing that he's in the drug business. She has to know what's going on. She may even be helping him in order to get even with her father." Milly dropped her hands and stepped back.

Inocencio was quiet for a long moment. At last he said slowly, "You are telling me that El Diablo and Yolanda's lover Ignacio are the same person."

"Right!"

"And you think that Señorita Yolanda is involved in growing and selling the marijuana."

"Right!" Milly looked away and shook her head in disgust. "How do you suppose that young woman can stand making love to such an awful man?"

"Gosh," said Inocencio, the pragmatist, "I guess business is business."

CHAPTER 21

By eleven-fifteen, the guests had gone to bed and all the other lights in the house were out except for the ones in room seven. Milly and Inocencio were in the cottage, in the dark, spying.

"Where are your sons, Inocencio? Are they hiding all through the garden?"

"Three of them are in the empty lot. I told them to follow whoever comes through the old door, but to be sure to stay out of sight. Another is just outside Yolanda's room, behind the pomelo tree, and the two nephews are back among the low branches of the banana palm."

"And Elpidio?"

"He's over by the front door."

Milly had Inocencio lift the suitcase down from her closet shelf. She opened it and groped for Herbert's old .38 caliber pistol. "Here," she said, "take this. There's a box of ammunition in here somewhere too."

Inocencio said, "Thank you. I feel a lot safer with this in my hand, but ay-yi it's dark out there and I hope I don't shoot one of my own boys by mistake!"

"Omigosh, I hadn't thought of that! Here, give it back!"

"No, I'm going to keep it. I'll be careful, don't worry."

"What do you mean, *don't worry?*" she said, and heard Inocencio giggle nervously.

"Señora, we've got everyone in place. Now all we can do is wait. Why don't you get some rest. I'll sit right here and keep an eye on things."

Milly took off her shoes and lay down on her bed. "I'll try to have a nap," she said, "but you have to promise to wake me up if anything happens."

"I promise."

As she pulled up her afghan against the chill of the night air she heard Inocencio settle into the rocking chair. But even with him on guard inside the room she felt shivers when she thought of El Diablo. Somehow, she could not think of him as Ignacio. Not yet.

Milly found that she was too keyed up to relax. She kept imagining El Diablo creeping through the garden. How could Inocencio's sons possibly subdue him when he was so big? The sons didn't seem to think it would be a problem—but they hadn't seen him yet. Inocencio did have Herbert's pistol; that was comforting. And Milly had a secret weapon: as a last resort, she could call Sergeant Ernesto Fuentes because she had memorized the number of the police station and there was a phone beside her bed.

The plan was for everyone to stay in hiding and let El Diablo go into Yolanda's room. When he came out again, tired and with his guard down, that was when they'd jump him. They expected to be so quiet about it that the other guests would not wake up during the fracas.

Milly couldn't see how that would work. However, there was one slim chance that the entire house would not be roused, simply because Leslie's family was in room twelve way over by the front door, Poul and Olga were in number three at the far end of the patio, and Elmer and Billie Jo were tucked away in room five beside the kitchen. If El Diablo didn't cry out, and if Inocencio's troops could operate in utter silence, they might get away with it, but in her estimation the odds were extremely poor.

Suddenly, the dog was barking. It was far too early, wasn't it? She sat up straight, straining to hear footsteps, but the hysterical barking drowned out all other sounds. When it finally stopped, she reached for her clock. "It-is-one-forty-seven-ayem," said the electronic voice.

This was it!

"Inocencio," she said quietly.

No answer.

She tossed the afghan aside and stood up, the tile floor cold against her stockinged feet. She padded over to the rocking chair and put out a hand to jiggle his shoulder and wake him. The chair was empty.

Her first reaction was anger that he had gone off without telling her, then anger quickly turned to fear as she realized that she was now all alone and vulnerable. What should she do? She cocked her head, waiting for Herbert to issue his usual instructions, but this time he didn't offer a blasted thing.

"Damn you, Herbie," she muttered. She lifted her chin bravely and whispered, "Well, okay...I'm on my own."

For a long time she stood just inside her screen door, peering out into the garden. She knew perfectly well that she couldn't see anything out there, but staring into the blackness made it easier to hear, for some idiotic reason. It was very still. The tree frogs and cicadas must be listening too, waiting for all the silly humans to quit sneaking about the garden and go home where they belonged.

Yolanda's voice drifted on the air, cutting through the darkness softly but with perfect clarity.

"¿Estás bien?" Are you all right? "You look terrible! Come on in here. We need to talk."

El Diablo replied in a soft rumble, the words unintelligible.

There was a tiny click and the voices dropped to the faintest of murmurs. A closed door and eighteen inches of adobe wall, thought Milly, could muffle almost anything.

She tried to picture what would happen when El Diablo came out of that room, and her imagination took off at a mad gallop. If he could get past the troops, he might head for her cottage. Once he walked through her door, there'd be no way she could escape from him. Immediately she felt claustrophobic and knew that she had to get out of here and into the outdoors. Anyway, she rationalized, she could hear better outside, and if she stayed close to the laundry room she'd be out of sight and in no one's way.

Her feet were freezing. She dug her old running shoes out of the closet, slipped into them and laced them tightly. Then hastily she took stock of her appearance: shoes and pants were dark, blouse a pale pink. She groped through the closet, found a navy blue jacket with a hood and put it on, pulling the hood up to cover her white hair. She moved back to the door, opened it, and slipped out into the night with a feeling of release. Impulsively, she bent over and smeared mud on her face like a World War II commando. Feeling a trifle foolish, but satisfied that she was now completely invisible, she moved to the corner of the laundry, flattened her body against the wall and held her breath, listening.

Slowly she became aware of quiet footsteps approaching along the path behind the laundry. She didn't dare call out to ask who it was. She was afraid to move, couldn't run. She stood like a statue and prayed that her camouflage would protect her.

The footsteps stopped close by. Something grabbed her hand. She gasped and jerked away.

"Shhh," whispered Leslie, "it's only me."

Jesus!

"What are you doing here?" she demanded in a fierce whisper. "Go back to bed!"

"All these people must be trying to catch the big guy who broke the trap, and I'm going to help."

"No you're not!"

"I've got it all set up. Don't worry."

"What do you mean, *don't worry!*"

Leslie didn't bother to answer. He just stood there. Milly's eyes closed and her shoulders slumped. She had to do something about this child. Leslie was a real pain, but if anything happened to him it would be terrible.

"Take my hand," she whispered, "and come with me. I need you to help me."

She led him around the corner and opened the door to the laundry room. The key was in the outside lock. Good. "There's a flashlight somewhere on the table behind the door," she said. "See if you can find it." The moment he was in, Milly stepped back outside, pulled the door shut and turned the key, all in one swift movement. Triumphantly, her heart pounding, she pulled the key out of the lock and dropped it into the deep pocket of her jacket.

Leslie rattled the doorknob, but he had sense enough not to shout.

She crept back to her wall and leaned against it. As her heart settled back to normal, she heard Herbert's voice inside her mind. *Shame on you, Mildred, you have just bamboozled an innocent child!*

Horsefeathers, she answered silently. *I probably saved his life! Anyway, where were you a while ago when I needed you?*

A sudden breeze rattled the fronds of the banana palm, and Milly thought of Inocencio's two nephews hiding there. It was hard to believe that there were eight men waiting at various spots around her garden. They were so quiet.

From then on, time passed slowly and eventually Milly grew bored. She was determined to stick it out no matter how long El Diablo stayed inside with Yolanda, but surveillance was turning out to be so tedious that she might have fallen asleep standing up except that her feet hurt. When the door to Yolanda's room finally opened and Milly heard voices again, it was so unexpected that she nearly jumped out of her skin. The usually strident El Diablo whimpered as Yolanda scolded him. Her voice was husky and very quiet, but the words were as incisive as a willow switch.

"After what you just told me about shooting my father and uncle, I will have nothing more to do with you. Help me? You have only helped yourself! You and I are no longer lovers. We're not even business partners anymore! Get out of my sight!"

What? Yolanda was a partner, too? Good grief.

"Help me, *querida*..."

"*Ni de loca*! Not even if I were crazy."

Milly heard the door close. Yolanda had shut him out of her room and, presumably, her life.

El Diablo groaned. Milly heard his shambling footsteps along the veranda, then a heavy whump like half a ton of bread dough falling. Immediately, all about her the silent garden erupted into movement as Inocencio and his boys rushed through the darkness to converge on the fallen El Diablo. One thing about her poor sight; she could see almost as well—or as poorly!—in the dark as she could in broad daylight, so she trotted boldly toward the fracas, her own garden path comfortably familiar underfoot.

Ahead of her she heard the sounds of heavy retching and moaning. A horrible odor filled the air. Whatever was going on with El Diablo had to be very serious. She slowed and stretched one hand out before her so she wouldn't run into anyone.

"Did you get him?" she whispered.

A sweaty little paw slipped into hers.

"Yes," whispered Leslie with obvious satisfaction, "we got him."

Milly drew back in amazement. "How did you get out of the laundry?"

"The window. Then I tied a piece of Inocencio's twine to the veranda pillar and tripped the big guy with it when he came out of Yolanda's room."

Milly grabbed Leslie by the shoulders, ready to shake the stuffing out of him. Herbert's voice said, *Forget it, Mildred.*

You know the kid has worn you down. Just accept him and try to love him. He needs it.

"I give up," she whispered, laughing silently, and gathered Leslie into a hug.

She felt someone else draw close to her in the dark. Inocencio's voice said quietly, "El Diablo is very sick, señora."

"Is that him vomiting?"

"Yes, but it is more than just an ordinary illness. I think he is dying. What should we do?"

Her first impulse was to tell him to fetch the doctor. Then she thought how foolish that would be.

"What's the matter with him?" she asked.

"He is throwing up all over the cement and he has terrible diarrhea and it is very hard for him to breathe."

She listened closely. "Yes, I can hear all that."

"Pee-yew! Ad sbell it too," said Leslie.

"It wouldn't surprise me if Yolanda had poisoned him," Milly suggested. "She's been oddly preoccupied ever since she began to realize what happened to her father."

El Diablo thrashed and retched. Then Milly heard grunts and erratic footsteps and judged that he had somehow struggled to his feet and was lurching about. She heard the table scrape across the cement, a chair overturn, heard him fall heavily again and flop around on the pavement.

The door to number seven jerked opened and Yolanda said nastily, "Be quiet out there, Ignacio! You're going to wake the whole house."

They all froze.

"Help me, querida, I'm dying!"

"Then die, but be quiet about it. Just don't come back here," she added, and closed her door.

Milly heard deep sighs and knew that all eight men had started breathing again.

Inocencio whispered decisively, "We cannot allow him to die inside these walls. There would be a great scandal, it would be in the papers and everyone here would be arrested."

Milly recognized the truth when she heard it, but she couldn't bring herself to throw any living human being out the door like a piece of trash. "We can't just put him out in the street to die, I don't care who he is!"

Juan's deep voice murmured from out of the darkness. "That is no longer a problem, Doña Milly."

"What do you mean?"

"He is dead, señora."

There was a long moment of collective silence. It was not out of respect for the deceased, Milly realized, it was merely that everyone was listening to make sure that El Diablo's stertorous breathing had actually stopped. It had. No question. The silence was followed by soft, barely discernible stirrings all around her—the sound of eight men crossing themselves with fervor.

"Now," Inocencio said briskly, "we must get him out of here. Maybe we can carry him in a blanket."

"The blanket would tear because he is so heavy," said Elpidio's voice. "What if we put him into my wheelbarrow?"

"Shhh, speak more quietly," Inocencio ordered in a harsh whisper. "We don't want the Señorita Yolanda coming out here again to make things worse than they are already. Elpidio, this man is far too big for the wheelbarrow. His hands and feet would drag on the pavement."

"I know what to do!" said Milly. "Por favor, Elpidio, bring my wheelchair. And cover the seat with that plastic tarpaulin in the garden shed."

Elpidio objected in a panicky whisper. "A fresh corpse is too limp to sit up, patrona. He'll slump to the side and the chair will fall over and I won't be able to get him back up because he's too heavy."

"Tie him in with twine," said Leslie matter-of-factly. "There's enough right here around this pillar to do the job."

Elpidio went off to find the wheelchair, but he walked slowly, dragging his feet, and Milly knew that he was terribly upset.

Surprisingly, Inocencio heaved a discouraged sigh. "Dios mío. Where should we take the body?" he asked.

Milly could hardly believe that Inocencio, the little dynamo, was fading. She knew it was three in the morning and they were all dog-tired, but he was her rock, her mainstay. This was no time for his energy to flag. It was a moment before she could gather her wits and attempt to perk him up.

"How about the railroad station?" she suggested. "It's only a few blocks from here and it's downhill all the way."

"Yes! That is a good idea," said Inocencio, sounding enormously relieved. "No one will be there this time of night. If we all go, we can prop him up on a bench outside the station house, exactly like he did that poor campesino at the Santo Tomás bus stop. If anyone sees us doing it, they'll think we're just a bunch of drunks helping a drunken friend. Here," he added, "you might as well take the pistol. I won't need it any longer."

"Is it loaded?"

"Yes, but the safety is on. Point it at the ground."

Nervously, Milly slipped the pistol into her jacket pocket and heard it clink against the key to the laundry room.

Inocencio said, "A moment ago we heard Señorita Yolanda tell El Diablo that they are no longer partners, which implies that they have been partners up to now. In that case, she is as guilty of those two murders and the attempted murder of her father as he is. Are we going to let her get on an airplane and go to Mexico City?"

"No," said Milly, "we're not."

"How can we stop her?"

"I was thinking that if the police were to find Yolanda at the railroad station with El Diablo's body, they might arrest *her* for his murder instead of us."

"Perfecto! Roberto can take her there in his taxi."

Roberto's voice murmured, "I'll park out in front of the Casa, Doña Milly, and wait for you to bring the señorita out the door."

"Yes, but how do I persuade her to go?" asked Milly. "Well, never mind; that's my job and I'll think of something, and then I'll call the police. What time do you want her there, Inocencio?"

"Better give us half an hour after we leave here, so we'll have plenty of time to transfer the body to the bench and get away before the police arrive."

"Okay. You get him down there, sit him up on the bench, and I'll do the rest. Here comes Elpidio with the chair."

They put the wheelchair on the veranda as close to El Diablo's body as possible. Even so, getting him off the ground and into the chair posed a terrible problem. All eight men grunted and heaved and pushed and prodded. Milly imagined that it must be like wrestling three hundred gallons of Jello into a two-hundred-gallon container. All she could do was keep out of the way and wring her hands. She hoped her poor wheelchair would survive El Diablo's great weight.

"You'd better leave Elpidio here with Leslie and me," she whispered to Inocencio. "Somebody has to clean up this mess on the veranda before daylight."

"Elpidio won't want to do that, señora. He'll be afraid of El Diablo's ghost."

"I know, but I'll stick with him and then he can stay inside the cottage with me until daylight. I think you should go with your boys." She put a hand on Inocencio's arm. "One more thing—this time *please* find me the moment you get back. Wake me if you have to. I want to know what happens."

CHAPTER 22

The big front door clicked shut behind the enormous corpse and its six escorts. Milly shoved the image of their grisly errand to the back of her mind and turned to her own immediate task of bolstering Elpidio's courage while he prepared to scrub the veranda.

To her disgust, Herbert chose this moment to chuckle and say, *Elpidio is afraid of El Diablo's ghost, Mildred, so do try to keep his spirits up.* Milly could only groan and roll her eyes. Herbert's puns had always been untenable.

She sent Elpidio on his reluctant way to find a bucket and scrub brush. She understood his terror. Nevertheless, cleaning the veranda was a job that had to be done before anyone saw the mess by daylight and questioned her about it.

"Leslie, do you have a watch?" she whispered.

"No."

"Then I'll have to get my clock."

Milly felt her way down the four veranda steps and across the small patio to her room. Her talking clock was a cube about the size of a child's building block, so it fit into the pocket of her jacket. With the pistol on one side and the clock on the other, the jacket rested heavy on her shoulders and the pockets bulged over her hips. No matter. As she returned to the veranda she reached into the left pocket, touched the top of the clock and heard the muffled metallic voice say, "It-is-three-eighteen-ayem."

"Who's that?" whispered Leslie.

"Shhh. There's a talking clock in my pocket. See if you can help Elpidio."

In Milly's experience, fear was often a great motivator. It seemed to work well for Elpidio who zipped through the clean-up in almost no time. Using a squeegee, he scraped what he could off the veranda into a bucket and sloshed it down the toilet in Milly's bathroom. Then he scrubbed the cement with soap and water and rinsed it thoroughly with the hose. Miraculously, Yolanda did not appear, and no one else awakened. If anyone had heard a noise, they probably thought Elpidio was up very late—or very early—watering the garden.

Milly sent Leslie to peek out the front door. He reported that Roberto was in place with his taxi. So far, so good. She checked her clock frequently, determined to keep to the timetable she had worked out in her mind.

Casa Colonial was close to the railway station, but the police were on the other side of town. Milly figured that if Ernesto Fuentes left the police station at 3:30 and Yolanda left Casa Colonial at 3:45, they should both arrive at the railway station at about 3:50. Meanwhile, Inocencio and the boys would have had the half hour they needed to get to the station and arrange the corpse on the bench. It would be a tight schedule, but she thought it would work.

At exactly 3:30 she left Leslie to look after Elpidio and went to her cottage where she closed the door and called police headquarters on the phone beside her bed.

"Ernesto, this is Doña Milly."

"Buenas noches, Doña Milly. Don Inocencio said that you might call. Do you need my help?"

"No, everything is all right here, Ernesto, but there is something you should look into down at the railway station. I don't want to talk about it on the phone, but I suggest that you go there at once."

Ernesto's voice grew a trifle cool. "Can you give me more information, Doña Milly? I really can't drop everything here at headquarters and drive across town just because you tell me to."

Oh, gawd. She'd forgotten that Ernesto had been alerted by Inocencio, so he would not allow her, a mere female, to modify those instructions. Milly poked the top of her clock, heard the minutes passing much too quickly, and swallowed her anger.

"I know how terribly busy you must be," she said sweetly, "and I hesitated to call, but I'm trying to avoid a scandal in my house. You see, one of our guests smuggled a very bad man into her room. Then they left together, and right now the two of them are in a taxi headed for the railway station. Inocencio thinks you should investigate this because of their connection to another very serious matter. He says there's sure to be a promotion in it for you, Ernesto."

"Promotion, Doña Milly?"

"Sí, Ernesto. As a woman I don't understand these things very well." She gagged, but only a little, and pressed on. "Inocencio assures me that this could be of the greatest importance to your career as a policeman." She paused. "Will you be leaving right away, Ernesto?"

"Immediately, Doña Milly!"

Milly touched her clock again. Three thirty four. Four minutes late already, thanks to machismo! Only eleven minutes to get Yolanda convinced, organized and into the taxi. Milly rushed across the patio, up the steps to the veranda and over to room seven. As she raised her hand to knock, the light in the room went out.

Milly tapped on the pebbled glass panel. "Yolanda," she murmured urgently, "open the door. I need to tell you something important."

The light came back on and in a moment the door opened.

Yolanda gasped, "Are you all right, Milly? What's the matter with your face?"

Milly blinked distractedly. "My face?"

"Yes. It's covered with black dirt."

What on God's green earth...ohhh! Suddenly Milly remembered her muddy commando camouflage. "Uh, well," she babbled in embarrassment, "it's a mud pack."

She took a deep breath and crossed her fingers behind her back in childish preparation for telling another out-and-out lie. "I just got a phone call from your mother. She and your father are now in the ambulance and on their way out of town, but they have stopped at the railway station and want you to meet them there before they go on."

"The railway station?" Yolanda said doubtfully. "I thought they'd left town hours ago."

"All I know is that Adriana phoned from the station and said they'll wait there for you. It's not very far from here, but the police escort won't let them linger more than a few minutes, so you'll have to hurry."

"I'll get dressed right away, Milly. Can you call me a taxi?"

"Immediately, Yolanda." No point in admitting that there was already a cab at the front door.

In a surprisingly short time Yolanda came out of her room and hurried down the orchid arbor to the entryway where Milly, Elpidio, and Leslie waited. Elpidio helped her into the taxi and stepped back.

All at once, Milly knew that she had to follow the drama to its bitter end. She simply could not go passively off to bed and wait for Inocencio's report.

"I'm coming with you," she announced and climbed into the car.

"Move over!" said Leslie, and crowded in beside her.

"I'm not staying here alone," declared Elpidio, and he shut the door to the house and got into the front seat with Roberto.

When they arrived at the railway station, Roberto

pulled up on the left side of the street, jumped out and opened the door for Yolanda. Before Milly could follow, Roberto slammed the door in her face, got back behind the wheel and threw the car into reverse.

"What are you doing?" demanded Milly as they careened backward down the street.

"Just one little moment, señora. I must get my taxi out of sight before the policía arrive."

When he stopped and opened the door again, Milly climbed out onto the sidewalk and felt Leslie take one of her hands, Elpidio the other.

"This is great," whispered Leslie. "We're like The Three Musketeers."

"Or The Three Stooges," muttered Milly.

Back where Yolanda had climbed out of the taxi there seemed to be a street light. It was not far away. Milly could spot the lamp on high, looming through a gap in her lace-doily eyesight, but its illumination was too feeble for her to see anything here on the ground. Without her familiar garden paths under foot she'd have to trust Leslie and Elpidio. They led her down the sidewalk toward the street light, then veered off into the bushes. There seemed to be a faint rustling all around her and she thought she heard people breathing.

"Where are we?" she murmured.

Inocencio's whisper came out of the darkness, making her jump. "We're not far from Yolanda. She's on the other side of this hedge. The boys and I are here with you."

"Did you have any problems?"

"A man came by and stopped to look at us. But the boys began to sing, and the man laughed and went on."

"He thought you were drunk."

"Yes."

Screams pierced the darkness.

"That was Yolanda," whispered Leslie unnecessarily. "She found the body. Oh, my gosh—she's whacking him on the head with her purse! *Geee...*"

There was a lull as Yolanda stopped for breath. Milly heard a tremendous thud. "What happened? Tell me!"

"The body fell over sideways and rolled off the bench onto the grass. Now she's kicking him and screaming at the top of her lungs."

Yolanda was having one of her tantrums. "You filthy murderer!" she screamed. "I hate you! How could we have been partners? You shot my father, you rotten *hijo de puta*! May you roast in hell through all eternity!"

"Don't listen, Milly," whispered Leslie, and put his hands over her ears.

"It's all right," whispered Milly. "I've heard worse."

The sound of Yolanda's voice went on and on, became scrambled with the doo-dah-doo-dah pulse of a klaxon as a police car pulled up.

Inocencio's voice said close to her ear. "Be quiet, now. We don't want the police to find us."

"Is it Ernesto Fuentes?"

"Yes, Ernesto and another man." After a moment he whispered, "They have picked up Yolanda and are carrying her between them to the police car. She's screaming and struggling."

It was just too horrible. "Don't look!" Milly said to Leslie. She pulled him close and fumbled to put her hands over his eyes.

"Cut that out!" whispered Leslie and shoved her away.

The screams turned to racking sobs, then to snuffles and finally stopped altogether. Inocencio murmured, "Yolanda is in the back of the police car now and Ernesto and his assistant are standing on the sidewalk. I wonder what they're waiting for."

In a few minutes Milly heard another car pull up, then quiet voices talking.

Inocencio whispered, "It's the hearse from Bañuet Funerales. Ernesto must have radioed for it." He laughed softly. "They're getting out the stretcher. I hope they're strong enough to pick up that body, because *we're* not going to help!"

199

❉ ❉ ❉

There was a slight logistical problem in getting home. Milly had come away without her key to The Casa, and there was not enough room in Roberto's taxi for Milly, Leslie, Elpidio, and the wheelchair plus Inocencio and all his boys. Inocencio handed Milly his key to the house and managed to flag down another cab, which just happened to be driven by one of his sons-in-law. Milly's group climbed into the second taxi, and everyone else crowded into Roberto's.

On the way home Leslie said, "Milly, what is all this about, really? Why would Yolanda kill her boyfriend? And what did she do to make him so sick?"

"I'm not sure that she killed him, Leslie. It's up to the police to sort that out. But we do know that the big man killed two people and he was threatening to harm Julia's family. Yolanda was his partner, so she was an accessory to the crimes. He shot Yolanda's father, too, and that's what finally got her so mad at him."

The response was typical Leslie. "Oh, boy!" he said. "I helped catch a murderer. Wait'll the kids back home hear about this!"

"You must promise me not to tell anyone, not even your mother, until you have left Mexico because you could get all of us into a lot of trouble. Promise?"

"I promise."

"I hope you mean it, Leslie, because if you tell, it will screw up my life forever and I could easily die in jail. And if *you* were to get stuck here in Mexico," she said, adding the clincher, "you'd never be able to tell your friends at home how you caught a murderer."

"Milly," he said solemnly, "I promise I won't tell. Scout's honor!"

The taxi delivered them to Casa Colonial, and they eased through the big front door and closed it behind them.

"Oh, my," whispered Milly, "it's good to be home!"

They made their way through the garden toward the cottage, holding hands. Milly was so tired that she stumbled and had to tell herself to pick up her feet. Even Leslie appeared to be winding down. Elpidio crowded close to his patrona for protection against the ghost he believed to be still lurking on the veranda. It had been a frightening time and Milly was exhausted, but now they could relax and put it all behind them.

All at once, the silence was shattered by the barking of the dog on the roof. The sound boomed down into the patio, striking Milly's ears like a physical blow. The shock was enormous and she barely managed not to burst into tears. How on earth could yet another bad person be coming through the old door and down the path in her vacant lot? Could there be one more partner in that hellish company after all?

The dog snarled and roared, then settled into a bout of savage, relentless barking. After a long time, a man yelled and the barking stopped. The silence was intense.

"It's the ghost," whispered Elpidio. "The dog knows it's here!"

For the merest instant, Milly believed him. Terrified, she clutched his arm, staring wide-eyed into the darkness, waiting for the specter to appear. Leslie edged closer and bumped against her, accidentally setting off the clock.

"Jesus!" said Milly.

Her right hand slipped into the other pocket where it curved around the butt of Herbert's pistol and her finger fell instinctively onto the trigger.

"Yow," they heard, "urrr-yeeeow!"

Leslie giggled. "Oh boy!" he whispered, dancing up and down. "We got him. We finally got him!"

"It is the cat, patrona," Elpidio explained in a happy whisper.

"Thank you for telling me that," Milly whispered back sarcastically. "I thought the trap was broken."

Leslie said, "It was, but I fixed it while the grownups were having their dumb old siestas. Personally, I haven't taken an afternoon nap since I was three years old."

Very soon, as Elpidio had predicted on the day they built the trap, the cat became quietly resigned to its fate. At the same time, Milly's knees stopped shaking. And miraculously, when she sent Leslie off to bed he actually went. Meekly. At last the night settled back into a comfortable silence. The tree frog peeped experimentally, then more bravely, and was joined by a cicada.

When Elpidio clutched Milly's hand she understood that he was still frightened of the ghost. She said kindly, "Please come with me, Elpidio. I want you to stay in my room until morning because I'm afraid to be alone."

She invited him to sleep on Herbert's bed, but Elpidio insisted quite nobly that he could protect her better by lying on the floor across the doorway. Milly wanted to tell him that any self-respecting ghost would float right over him, but she was too tired to argue. She just handed him a blanket and a pillow, then kicked off her shoes and slid under the covers of her own bed without even getting undressed.

And then it was morning and the breakfast bell was ringing. Milly rolled over and called sleepily for Elpidio, but he was gone. She could hear him outside, as usual, watering the garden. She was alone and the sunshine poured through her windows.

Milly sat up on the side of the bed, engulfed by a monumental weariness. She folded her hands between her knees and stared toward her toes. After only three and a half hours of sleep, she had to fight her way through the pea-soup fog clouding her memory. Why had she called for Elpidio just now? And why did she still have her clothes on? One by one, the events of last night crept out of the murk and back into her consciousness, and with them came a strengthening flutter of excitement.

Quickly, she peeled off her clothes and stood under the shower, turning her face up to the spray, hoping it would clear her head as it washed away the mud camouflage. Then, feeling a little more like herself, she dressed and went out the door, heading for the dining room and a cup of coffee.

She was outside the kitchen, coffee cup in hand, when she heard the doorbell. Since she had borrowed Inocencio's key last night, he was probably standing out there ringing to get in. She forced her tired body into a semblance of its usual fast trot and headed for the entryway, her coffee sloshing in the cup.

"Buenos días, Doña Milly, are you all right this morning?"

"I'm fine, Inocencio. How are you? Did you and the boys get home all right? We'd have had a real mess here if they hadn't come to help us. Please thank them for me."

"De nada, señora, and we got home without any problem, thank you."

"Have you had word from Ernesto Fuentes?"

"No. I will be very surprised if Ernesto calls. I think that he will never mention the arrest to you or me."

"Why not?"

"He will pretend to himself that he was acting on his own, and he'll tell the Chief of Police that he got a hot tip from one of his own informants."

"Yeah, me!"

"That's all right. I hope he takes all the credit and leaves us out of it."

"Actually," said Milly, "I hope so, too." She took a gulp of coffee and set her cup on the desk. "I want to check Yolanda's room to see what she left behind. Will you come with me?"

"Of course, señora."

Milly gave an involuntary groan as she turned to walk down the orchid arbor. Every muscle in her body seemed to ache. "My gosh, what a night. I can't think when I've ever been so tired." She found it impossible to move with her usual pep, but Inocencio, too, seemed quite willing to walk slowly this morning. When they finally hobbled onto the veranda she asked, "How does it look? Did Elpidio do a good job?"

"Yes, the veranda is spotlessly clean."

He opened the door to room eight and they began their inspection. The room was neat. Nothing had been left behind. In room seven they found all the Sánchez suitcases packed and standing just inside the door, ready to go to the airport. Milly sat down on the nearest bed and closed her eyes. "Be sure to check the closet and all the drawers."

"Yes, yes; I know what to do. Oh, here's a note addressed to you. It's leaning against a really wonderful carved wooden angel."

"Why for goodness' sake. Read it to me, will you please?"

"'Dear Milly'," it began, "'Thank you for your many kindnesses to my parents and me. I have told this special angel that he must stay here and watch over you. Please hug him once in a while and think of your friend, Yolanda, who loves you.'"

Milly's jaw dropped. "Well I'll be damned!" she said.

"Señora, I don't want to feel sorry for that despicable young woman, but I can't help it."

"I know what you mean, Inocencio. I feel sorry for her, too. I even *like* her. She's bright and loving, but she's also cruel and unstable and...well, she's a criminal."

"Yes. Her parents always loved her, but they didn't know how to help her. It's a terrible waste."

Milly nodded in understanding. Inocencio, of all people, would reduce this complex issue to one of simple child rearing. He had done an amazing job of teaching honor and integrity to his own thirteen youngsters, and he and Lidia had struggled to bring out the potential in each of them. Inocencio might not know it consciously, but his family was his true life's work.

"I suspect that Yolanda's problem is at least a couple of generations deep," she said. "Her background was pretty strange. For one thing, when she was thirteen, she found the body of her sister who had been brutally assaulted and murdered. That was bound to leave its mark on her."

"That is terrible. But worse things have happened to people without turning them into hard-boiled criminals and accessories to murder."

Milly nodded. "You're right. But of course it's never just one thing that changes a person, and we don't know what else happened to her. I do know that while her immediate family was suffocatingly close and outwardly loving, they didn't give two whoops for anyone else on the planet."

"How do you know that?"

"Just think about it; they didn't care that they ruined thousands of lives by dealing drugs. For them it was just 'business.' And her father and uncle and lover thought nothing of killing someone like Paco or harming his children; it was just 'business.' Their values were terribly skewed, and Yolanda grew up in that atmosphere."

"And yet she was tender and loving toward you, señora."

"Oh, yes. I believe she regarded me as a grandmother. In her mind, I was 'family.' But if she knew that I had set her up for arrest, I'll bet she wouldn't hesitate to have me killed."

With a sad little smile Milly laid the angel beside her on the bed. "I'll keep this in memory of the Yolanda I thought I knew," she said. "It will remind me that there's some good in everyone."

As Inocencio continued his inspection Milly thought about Rodolfo Sánchez and wondered if he'd survived the trip to Mexico City. She had no idea how much Adriana knew about the family business. Perhaps that lady had chosen to walk through life with her eyes shut.

While Inocencio opened and closed drawers, Milly ran her hands back and forth on top of the bedspread, distracting herself with the feel of the rough weave against her palms. She came across an oddly smooth pebble lying there, and then another. She picked them up, stroking their cool surfaces with the tips of her fingers.

"What are these?" she asked, curious. "At first I thought they were stones, but they're too lightweight for that."

Inocencio came closer. "Those are castor beans," he said. "Where did you find them?"

"They were lying right here on the bed."

"Put them back immediately, señora. Castor beans are very poisonous."

Milly dropped the beans as if they were hot coals and went into the bathroom to wash her hands. "I told you last night that Yolanda had poisoned El Diablo," she called over the sound of water running in the basin.

Still, as she dried her hands, something niggled at the back of her mind. She recalled hearing somewhere that castor beans often took several days to do their work. One could not force a castor bean into a victim's mouth in anger and have him die immediately. Castor bean poisoning would require some fairly long-term planning. Had Yolanda been that angry with El Diablo before last night?

Inocencio said, "Ernesto Fuentes will probably come by later today to pick up the suitcases, and he'll want to search these two rooms for himself. I'll tell Ramona not to clean them until he has been here."

Milly got the message. "I guess I'll just leave the castor beans here on the bed," she said casually.

"Whatever you say, señora," Inocencio replied.

Something in his voice made Milly picture him with a secretive smile on his face.

CHAPTER 23

Paco Soriano López stood under the cork oak tree, leaning on his hoe and gazing out across his cornfield. It was too soon after sowing for new plants to have carpeted the earth with green. But as he walked the rows, here and there he found tiny pale green shoots thrusting between the clods, stretching toward heaven and life-giving sunlight.

The corn was showing; the marijuana was not. It had been planted a day later than the corn, so perhaps it would appear tomorrow or the next day. Paco felt a thing like a cold fist grab at the middle of his chest when he thought of having to coax the marijuana out of the earth and into their lives. If only El Diablo would die soon!

"Papá! Papá!"

Paco spun around and saw Juan running toward him along the side of the field. What terrible thing had happened now? Shaking with fear, Paco threw down his hoe and hurried to meet his son.

"What is wrong, mi hijo?"

"Nothing is wrong, Papá, but Mamá says you are to come quickly."

They started for home, half-walking half-running. "Tell me what is happening," urged Paco.

"I'm not supposed to tell you, Papá, but I will say this much: it's good news."

They hurried through the gate and Paco slowed in confusion. Grandfather, Amelia and the children were gathered around Doña Milly and an anglo boy who held a clumsy-looking box made of bamboo slats fastened together. Don Porfirio, the brujo, stood nearby appearing stern and important. What was he doing here?

Amelia looked straight at Paco, her face expressionless, but her eyes aglow. "My husband," she said, "Doña Milly has brought us interesting news. Do you remember the big man you saw in the hammock at Casa Colonial? The one with the purple shoelaces?"

"I remember."

"He died last night and the police have arrested his murderer."

The fist in Paco's chest unclenched and his body felt liquid, dizzy, as if warm mezcal were pouring through his veins. He thought to himself, *We are all saved, gracias a Dios.* He shut his eyes for one blissful moment, then opened them wide. He needed to hear it again. "Are you sure he's dead, Doña Milly?"

"He died at my house, Paco, so I'm sure. At this very moment his body is at the mortuary."

"I would not wish death to any man, señora, but I confess that I am relieved. El Diablo was wicked."

The brujo lifted one hand in a pompous gesture. "Our righteous God will punish him appropriately," he intoned.

"In that case," said Grandfather, "El Diablo must be dancing in the fire at this very moment—and he's probably selling marijuana to his namesake!"

The Anglo boy laughed loudly. Then he stepped toward Paco and said, "Señor, I have brought Julia a present; something to remember me by when I go back to California. I hope you'll allow her to keep it." He set the bamboo container on the ground at Paco's feet.

Paco leaned forward to peer between the slats. "It's a

cat," he said, lifting his eyebrows in surprise.

Julia said, "It's a very handsome cat, Papá. May I keep it, please?"

"I don't know," said Paco. A pet was a luxury and they could not afford luxuries. On the other hand, it might be indelicate to turn down a gift from one of Doña Milly's friends. "Ask your mother," he said, passing the decision to Amelia.

"I'm not sure, Paco..."

The grandfather said firmly, "Of course you may keep the cat, Julia. It will be part of our family." They all turned to stare at him. "And since everyone in our family shares the work of the household, the cat's job will be to catch the mice that steal our corn."

"Terrific!" said Leslie. "And I give you permission to name the cat after me," he added with a magnanimous sweep of his arm. "I don't know whether the cat is a boy or a girl, but the name Leslie is appropriate for either one."

"Ahh," said Grandfather, nodding wisely. "Unisex!"

Doña Milly giggled; a bit wildly, Paco thought. He knew that she too was relieved to be free of El Diablo. "Amelia," she said, "I would like to buy the blue runner for the center of the table—the one to match the blue place mats—if you still have it."

"Of course, Doña Milly. It will be my gift to you."

After everyone left, Paco said, "Amelia, there are still one or two hours of daylight left. Before suppertime we can probably replace at least one row of marijuana with corn. Are you willing?"

"Of course, *mi esposo*," Amelia replied, and her eyes sparkled as she smiled her gentle smile.

They walked toward the cornfield, scuffing their toes in the warm dust. Paco's entire world seemed brightened by his relief and happiness. The cooing of the doves was like a song of love. The scraggly copal trees seemed leafy and full, the countryside lush. His castor beans were vigorous. The maguey plants flourished, their leathery leaves plump and pointed.

Once again, contentedly, Paco looked to the hills. Rank after rank of high mountains marched into the endless mists. He shifted his gaze to Amelia, returning her smile as the late afternoon sun warmed her dear face with its glow.

AUTHOR'S NOTES

Santo Tomás Jalieza is a real village; a small collection of families who scrabble for a living while adhering firmly to their ancient heritage of pride and honor. The village women are fine weavers and strong characters; the men are equally stalwart, honest and hard-working.

For the purposes of this story, I have peopled Santo Tomás entirely with imaginary folk. These "Book People" are able to work through a frightening, completely imaginary situation because they possess all of the fine qualities of the real people after whom they are modeled.

Casa Colonial is a real guest house in the heart of Oaxaca City. The characters of Milly and Herbert are based very loosely on my parents who founded Casa Colonial and began their grand Oaxaca adventure in the seventies.

Qué descansen en paz, may they rest in peace.

❀ ❀ ❀

CASA COLONIAL RECIPES

STUFFED CHAYOTES

6 chayote squash
6 tbsps butter
1 med onion finely chopped
2 tsp chopped parsley
2 cloves garlic minced
1/2 cup golden raisins
12 olives pitted and sliced
salt and pepper
2 med. tomatoes, simmered 3 minutes, peeled
and chopped

Cook the chayotes whole in boiling salted water until just tender. Drain, cool, cut in half lengthwise. Remove pulp with a spoon, leaving a shell about half an inch thick. Set shells aside.

STUFFING:Saute onion and garlic in the butter until translucent. Add all other ingredients plus the pulp you scooped out of the chayotes, and simmer until thick. About 20 minutes. Salt and pepper to taste.

Fill chayote shells with the vegetable stuffing, top with buttered bread crumbs and a dry, grated cheese. Bake at 350 degrees for 20-30 minutes to heat thoroughly.

GRACIELA'S STRAWBERRY PIE

Crust
1 cup flour
1/4 cup powdered sugar
1/2 cup margarine
Sift flour and sugar together. Blend in margarine. Push into a 9" pie pan, across the bottom and up the sides. Prick all over with a fork and bake at 350 for 10 minutes. Cool.

NOTE: Graciela prefers to use an ordinary pastry pie shell, cooled. Both are good.

Filling
2 small (regular sized) baskets of strawberries.
Fill cooked pie shell with strawberries which have been washed, stemmed and dried. Arrange the berries pointy-end up so they look attractive.

Glaze
1 1/2 cups water
1 package wild strawberry Jello
3/4 cups sugar
2 tblsp cornstarch
Mix water, sugar and cornstarch thoroughly in a saucepan and place over high heat, stirring constantly until glaze "clears" and comes to a boil. Remove from heat and quickly add the package of Jello, stirring until Jello is dissolved. Spoon over the berries in the pie shell, coating each berry with the glaze. Pour in the rest of the glaze until the pie shell is filled. Refrigerate. Serve with whipped cream.

Mary Madsen Hallock has spent most of her life in California, but fell in love with the huge Colonial city of Oaxaca when it was still a sleepy provincial capital of some twelve thousand souls. Ten years later she became owner of the real Casa Colonial and led more than fifty groups of tourists to the area. She now resides in Santa Rosa, California, and is hard at work on *Ghost of a Gringo*, the second book in the Casa Colonial mystery series. She is still in regular contact with her Zapotec friends in Oaxaca.